WHiP 3

Whip's Extreme Adventure

The Third Whip Book by

Tyler Johns

Order this book online at www.trafford.com
or email orders@trafford.com

Most Trafford titles are also available at major online book retailers.

Print information available on the last page.

ISBN: 978-1-4907-7549-4 (sc)
ISBN: 978-1-4907-7548-7 (hc)
ISBN: 978-1-4907-7550-0 (e)

Library of Congress Control Number: 2016912053

Trafford rev.   07/27/2016

 www.trafford.com

North America & international
toll-free: 1 888 232 4444 (USA & Canada)
fax: 812 355 4082

CONTENTS

Foreword ix

Chapter 1   Back With the Whip Team 1
Chapter 2   Whip Babysits 5
Chapter 3   Packing Up 9
Chapter 4   Off to College 11
Chapter 5   Tehran's Job Loss 15
Chapter 6   The Moves, Part 1 17
Chapter 7   Meet the Arctics 19
Chapter 8   Back to College for Tehran 24
Chapter 9   The Regular Classes 25
Chapter 10   Father and Son Together Again 27
Chapter 11   The Mystic Four 28
Chapter 12   The Next Day 35
Chapter 13   Spare Time in the Library 37
Chapter 14   Draco Malfunction 39
Chapter 15   Ratman and Bobbin 41
Chapter 16   The Moves, Part 2 43
Chapter 17   The Shoe Gone Quazy Club 46
Chapter 18   The Saturday Night Dance 49
Chapter 19   The Karaoke Concert 52
Chapter 20   Another Week Goes By 60
Chapter 21   The College Amusers 62
Chapter 22   Mobi and Maudi's Suspension 67

Chapter 23   A Hard Time For a Father and Son.................................. 69

Chapter 24   Lab Brats 72

Chapter 25   Tehran's Guilt..74

Chapter 26   A New Plan for the Whip Team 76

Chapter 27   Getting the Grades Up 78

Chapter 28   Tehran Quits the Arctics.. 80

Chapter 29   Championship Time... 83

Chapter 30   The Big Competitions.. 84

Chapter 31   The Bad Start... 88

Chapter 32   The Triathlon Goes On... 91

Chapter 33   Close to the Finish Line... 96

Chapter 34   The Trophy... 98

Chapter 35   The End of the Year 100

Amusers' Idol 103

Notice: If you read the previous stories about Whip, Bobi, and Pition, get a load of their busted moves in this one when they all go to college and meet some of the funniest human beings and animals (even the sexiest ones in town) that you'll get to know.

FOREWORD

You probably know the story of the Mythical creature, psyvark, known as Whip. It all started with him and his two reptilian friends, Bobi, a crocodile, and Pition, a python. They chit chatted with their friends in high school.

On summer vacation, Whip and his family went to the eastern outer part of Virginia to visit their anteater friends, the Andor family. Then later they met with Tehran's brother, Seth, and father, Ebenezer. Ebenezer told a story about invading pirates called the Vips. The Vip king Brendor, wanted to rob the market. The animals from the Vips' truck ran to Whip's neighborhood to tell Whip, Bobi, and Pition about the robbery. And so, they defeated the Vips and the police paid them a large reward. It was enough money for them to do whatever they wanted.

Then Whip built an invention vehicle called the World Bug 3000. What he didn't know about was that Brendor's daughter, Zelda, would disappear without love. So she did. And so, the whole Vip case was closed.

In the second book, Whip, Bobi, and Pition heard the story about a Siberian white tiger dynasty called, the Satvrinskis. The mother was Tsarina Abmora, and her son was Prince Aborabor. They had an evil plan to make Whip's kid sister, Sarah Psy, a smart creature like her brother. It was up to Whip to save her from such disaster. He got help from a walrus named, Fentruck Tusker, who knew about the white tigers. He became Whip's roommate at the end of that story.

Now let's get on to the third story…

CHAPTER 1

Back With the Whip Team

It was the summer of 2002, Whip, Bobi, and Pition had finished their last year of high school. They were all equally ready for college. They even had enough money from the reward they had received from the police for solving the Vip case in their first adventure.

Anyway, Whip was riding on his Christmas present skateboard on the half pipe in his backyard. Pition was practicing his dodging ability with the sprinkler. Bobi was jumping over small hurdles on a pair of rollerblades. Fentruck was running on an exercise machine for a weight loss. He was prepared to aid the three main guys in college.

Whip's father, Tehran, was putting up a sign saying "Good Luck at COLLEGE, BOYS". He taped the top corners on the top frame of the back door. Pition's father, Pittz, wore his robot suit with arms and legs and cooked the hamburger patties on the barbecue. He grabbed the spatula with his robot arm and flipped the patties as soon as they were ready.

Back as the boys were doing moves, Whip did a standing trick on one end of the half pipe, grabbing the ledge. His skateboard was on his feet pointing up. Then he skated to the other end and stopped to sit on the top wall. The other guys stopped what they were doing.

"Going off to college means no more casualties," Whip said.

"And we have to find some majors," said Pition.

"We'll never know what to be, though," said Bobi.

"We'll be in a big competition for…" said Whip.

"…THE COLLEGE AMUSERS!" the guys all said together.

"We're the geniuses ought to save our world," said Whip.

"The first team to put those Arctic guys on their tailed booties!" said Bobi shaking his tail. He skated with his rollerblades across the half pipe. He sat on the ground to take them off.

"New plan, guys!" Whip called out. "We need a sprinkler and a toy."

Bobi went to get a five-nozzle sprinkler from the side of the house. He brought it by the side of the half pipe. He attached the garden hose to it. Pition got an old rag doll that Whip's sister, Sarah, must have thrown out in the dirt. He got some tape and strapped the doll to Whip's skateboard. He coiled it in his body and grappled up to the top of the half pipe's end. He swung the board up there and got his body up. Whip went to the hose faucet and put his hand over the turning handle.

"Smart thinking," said Fentruck walking by.

"Is the sprinkler all set?" Whip asked Bobi.

"All set and ready to rip," Bobi said.

"Doll on board ready?" Whip asked Pition.

"Ready or not, here it comes," Pition said.

"Here goes nothing," said Whip as he turned the handle. The sprinkler was activated with spraying nozzles of water launched over the half pipe. The sprinkler's metal tube pivoted back and forth. Pition released the skateboard and it rolled down the ramp and to the other end.

"The plan is a success," said Whip.

Some of the sprinkler's water was sprayed on the board and the doll. Whip grabbed his board and unstrapped the doll and tossed it away.

And so, as Pittz cooked the food on the barbecue, Tehran set the outdoor table with a cloth and paper plates, including plastic cups, forks, and knives. After he finished setting everything, he went by Pittz.

"So, Pittz," he started talking, "one time you were saying that your son graduated in a sly sort of way…"

"He was no ordinary snake in the grass," said Pittz. "Just think. I'll be a free snake when I'm through with my job! Oh yeah!" He giggled with his forked tongue wiggling. He slid out of his robot suit. His snake body was merely stretched out.

"I suppose," said Tehran.

Meanwhile, Whip, Bobi, and Pition saw their lunch pal from high school, Gavin, a human kid. He rode on his skateboard by the sidewalk wearing his bicycle helmet. He held a reading book in his hand.

"Yo, Gavin!" Bobi called to him, raising his hand. "Long time, no see."

"Hey, guys!" Gavin said as he approached the animals, standing by the fence. "I heard you're all going to college together."

"We sure are," said Bobi.

"We've been accepted to the Appalachian University in Harrisonburg, Virginia," said Whip.

"Well good luck, guys," said Gavin.

"What's that book you're reading?" Pition asked him.

"It's called *Us,*" said Gavin. "It's about a person telling the story talking about himself and all the creatures in the world. The author's name is George Larraby."

"Well, good luck on that book," said Bobi.

"Cool," said Gavin. "I guess we'll bump into each other next vacation when you guys get out for any reason."

"I guarantee it," said Whip.

Gavin walked on his skateboard and rolled away to his home.

And so, as Pittz cooked many hamburger patties, he turned to Tehran and said, "Hey, Teh, why don't you get the boys? Lunch is just about ready."

The guys came by the table and took a seat on the plastic chairs.

"So where's the food?" asked Bobi. "I'm starving."

"I'm not even that hungry to swallow a whole loaf of salami," said Pition.

"I can eat a plain patty," said Bobi.

"Here you go, boys," said Pittz as he brought the plate of patties and set it in the middle of the table.

Bobi grabbed a various number of plain patties. Pition grabbed one. Whip took two and put them on buns. He took some leaves of lettuce and a few tomato slices. He ate each part one by one. Bobi stacked three patties and ate them in one bite between his jaws. Pition swallowed his patty whole.

"I'm done eating for the week," he said. Then he slithered off his chair and out on the ground.

"You know," said Fentruck. "I've never eaten land food before. All I could eat were shellfish and barnacles."

"Try some food, Fen," said Whip. "It's good."

"Kind of greasy," said Bobi.

"Okay," said Fentruck. He took a bun and a patty just to eat a plain hamburger. He tried eating it. "Hmm," he said. "Delicious." He swallowed that bite. "My dog, Chewbacca, probably eats this stuff."

"Your dog 'Chewbacca'?" Whip asked.

"I named him after that Wookiee from the original *Star Wars,*" said Fentruck.

"Wowzers!" said Bobi. His cell phone rang in his left hip pocket. "Oop! Got a call." He answered it.

"Bobert!" it was his mother, Harley.

"Yes, Mama," Bobi said.

"Your brothers have risked another day on the park today," his mother said.

"Okay," said Bobi, "I'm coming." He hung up. "I'll see you later, guys. My mom's having a mental malfunction."

"By the way," said Whip. "I've got babysitting tonight with some koalas. I need to call that guy again." He got up from the table and took his cell phone out of his hip pocket. He walked on the grass and dialed a number that he was given. As soon as the call was answered, a koala spoke to Whip, saying, "Hello."

"Mr. Givington," Whip said, "what time do you want me to be at your house tonight for your kids?"

"At 6:00," said the koala.

"Alright," said Whip.

"My wife and I will be out on our date when you come by."

"Got it." Whip hung up.

Lunch was over. Pition and Pittz went back home. Tehran went inside the house. Fentruck went into his shack that he built by the Psys' backyard. Whip walked into the house to wait for the right time to babysit young koalas at their house.

CHAPTER 2

Whip Babysits

And so, Whip told his parents that he had babysitting that upcoming evening. He walked to the front door and waited for the right time. It was five minutes to 6:00. Whip went to the garage and started his invention, the World Bug 3000, to run. He drove it out and located a street called, Mumba Avenue, there in Psyville, on the monitor. He allowed the vehicle to hover toward the sky. Rocket boosters on the feet boosted up a few yards. Whip started the burning engine. He flew over town and as he aimed for Mumba Avenue, he launched the vehicle toward it. There was a neighborhood of Australian wild animals that had moved to that town of Psyville. Whip landed the World Bug in front of a tall, towering house, decorated with vines. Whip walked out of the vehicle and straight across the front yard's walkway. He knocked on the door. Then a koala answered it and opened it.

"Hello there," he said.

"Are you the one who called me?" asked Whip.

"Yes," said the koala. "Come on in."

Whip followed the koala inside. The koala led him into the living room to show him the pictures of his family on the piano. He showed each family member one by one, pointing his finger.

"My name is Leopold Givington," the koala introduced himself. "That's me in this picture…" He started pointing to his family picture. "…that's my wife, Millie, and our twin offspring, my son, William, my daughter, Agatha…" he showed other pictures of relatives on the walls nearby. "…and here is my brother, Augustus, and that's my sister, Debruary."

"Debruary?" Whip said. "That rhymes with the month, February."

"Right," said Mr. Givington. "My mother invented that name herself."

And so, the rest of the Givington family came by. Whip discovered the young twin koalas.

"So you're somebody's children I was hired to babysit," said Whip.

"And you are some strange creature we've never seen before," said the koala son, William.

"What are you supposed to be?" asked the koala daughter, Agatha.

"I'm a mythical creature, known as the 'psyvark'," Whip said. "I'm a psychic animal who collects the genius of man."

"Wow, that's mystical," said William.

"Well, I hope you take care of our young," said Mrs. Givington. "Your name?"

"Whip," Whip said. "Whip Psy."

"We'll be out on our date," said Mr. Givington. He and his wife went out the front door. They left in a small car and drove away.

And so, Whip started the babysitting job by resting on the couch thinking of his wisdom. William and Agatha snacked on the eucalyptus leaves that grew on a potted tree. Whip came up with an idea. He got a blank sheet of white paper from a printer on a living room desk that belonged to Mr. Givington, and got a pencil and started writing some ideas to start a career from college. He wrote:

Teacher

Scientist

Philosopher

Scholar

Geologist

Astronaut

Suddenly, Agatha came by with a toy train that she broke while playing in the other room.

"Whip," she said. "Can you fix this train? I broke it while playing with it."

"Well, sure," said Whip as he took the broken toy train. "I'm a professional." He used his psychic powers to locate broken sections he repaired the toy by hand. He put the wheels on the thin metal rod. Then he finished it.

"There you go," Whip said as he gave the toy back to Agatha.

"Thank you," said Agatha. "You really are a big help."

Whip decided to take a tour around the house. By the kitchen was a giant tank of water with a porcupine fish, an eel, and a seahorse swimming among leaf-shaped seaweed that looked as it came from a tropical rain forest. There was an elevator that would take an inhabitant of the house up the next two floors. Whip looked through a spy hole in the floor. The basement was a science lab. William always worked in there with chemicals and machines. Whip climbed on the elevator and pushed a button that said "B" for basement. The elevator lowered him down to that lab below and met William using a microscope on a metal table, looking at a slide with his own saliva mixed in iodine.

"Wow," said Whip. "I never thought about kids with a lab under their house, except on TV."

"Yep," said William as he got up when he was done with the microscope. "I'm trying to grow up to be a genius like you."

"Really?" said Whip. "How exciting. I'm going to college with my friends pretty soon."

"Wow," said William, "you're getting old. What are you going to study? My dad told me I should study something when I grow up."

"I'm not sure," said Whip. "It's quite complicated." He climbed back on the elevator. "I'll see around, William."

"You can call me 'Will'," said William. He went back to his experiment.

Whip rode the elevator back up to the first floor. He met Agatha with a board game held in her hands.

"Whoa, hey, Agatha," Whip said in surprise as the elevator opened.

"You can call me 'Aggie'," said Agatha. "How about a game?"

"No thanks," said Whip, "I'm okay without one."

"I don't like playing alone," said Agatha. "But I'll try it."

Whip went back to resting on the couch. Agatha played that board game alone with two pieces on the kitchen table.

Will and Aggie, Whip thought, those cubs sure are the good kind.

And so, a while later, Mr. and Mrs. Givington returned home from their date. Whip got off the couch and confronted the koala parents.

"How were our offspring?" asked Mr. Givington.

"They were nice and good at behaving," said Whip.

"I predicted that myself," said Mrs. Givington.

"I should be going home now," said Whip.

"So long, boy," said Mr. Givington waving his hand as Whip walked out the door.

As Whip went back into the World Bug 3000, night was neigh and the young koala twins were happy to see their parents. Whip flew back home.

CHAPTER 3

Packing Up

Whip parked the vehicle in the garage. He went back into his house. His mother, Corbin, approached him.

"How was babysitting, Whip?" she asked.

"It was normal," said Whip. "They were good for me."

"Well, wonderful," said Corbin.

"I gotta get packed for college," Whip said.

"Well it's just a few days away."

Whip walked up to his bedroom. In the television room, his kid sister, Sarah, was doing a sign game with her stuffed toy dragon, Fredwick.

In the last story, Sarah lost control of her bladder in school when it reached winter vacation. But afterwards, she had a doctor's appointment that gave her a shot so that she could control her bladder again.

As Whip entered his room, he grabbed a snap-lock suitcase out of his closet. He packed numerous shirts, pants, and socks. He got his toothbrush and a paste tube along with a stick of deodorant from the bathroom. For the case of boredom, he packed a dartboard from his bedroom wall. Suddenly, Whip's father entered the room.

"Is everything quite organized?" he asked.

"Yep," said Whip. "Man, I can't wait to get out of here." He ceased packing.

"Here, let me help you pack," said Tehran.

"Dad," said Whip, sighing. "It's okay, I've got everything settled." He went to his dresser and packed a few pairs of pajamas.

"I see you have a good set of clothing that fits you well," said Tehran. "You need a laundry hamper."

"That's what I'm looking for," said Whip. He went back in the closet and got a net with tiny holes in the string hatched surface. He packed it in his suitcase. He snapped his case shut.

"Well then," said Tehran. "I've got something for you right here." He walked back to the doorway and lifted up a heavy box. He gave it to his son as a gift. Whip gently handled the box and set it on his lap as he sat on his bed.

"Man this thing weighs a ton," Whip whimpered. "Hey, I'll bet it's one of those machines for computer generators for power, man they're so cool." He opened the box. Inside was an antique typewriter. Tehran grabbed his camera from his hip pocket and took a photograph.

"What do you think, son?" he asked.

"Nothing," said Whip. "It's just an old, old typewriter. Uh, where'd you get it?"

"It was my father's since I was a teenager," said Tehran. "And now, son, I'm giving it to you."

Whip mumbled under his breath. "Thanks, Dad," he said.

"You know, when you're in college, you will have a dormitory and you're gonna make some kind of major."

"Right."

"And it's going to be quite a long time before, perhaps next Christmas."

"Don't worry, Dad, it'll go by however long it lasts. I'll be in there for the next three years."

Tehran went by the door and put his finger over the light switch.

"Monday's going to be the big day," Whip said as he tucked himself in bed.

Tehran turned off the light. He closed the door but left it open an inch. He looked inside at his son with tears in his eyes that he would miss him as he went to college. So then he closed the door and went to bed as his son slept.

CHAPTER 4

Off to College

As the days went by, Bobi, Pition, and Fentruck did the same thing, getting ready for college, packing suitcases and all they needed.

And so, Monday morning arrived. A human boy on a bicycle threw newspapers to each house. Whip got out of bed. He got his suitcase and skateboard. Tehran was making breakfast. Corbin read the newspaper on the kitchen table.

"Did you brush your teeth, Whip?" asked Tehran.

Whip got a cup of orange juice from the refrigerator. He drank it up.

"Yes, Dad," he answered his father.

"Did you pack enough of what you need?" Tehran asked.

"Yes, I sure did," Whip answered.

"Did you put on deodorant?"

Whip sighed harshly as he was about to head for the front door with his luggage.

"Yes, Dad, I did everything," he answered his father.

"Yo, Whip!" Bobi called from outside.

"We have a road trip to make!" Pition called.

"Oop," said Whip. "I gotta go. Bye, Mom and Dad!" He dashed to the front door.

"Whip, wait!" Tehran followed his son.

Whip hurled out of his house and tossed his luggage to the roof of a new van that Bobi rented for a lot of money from a car shop. Bobi dodged Whip's luggage as it hit the roof. Pition grabbed the elastic cords with hooks to hold the guys' luggage on the roof. Bobi got into the driver's seat. Pition slithered through an open window on the side. Bobi started the van. Whip sat in the seat next to the driver.

"Are you going already?!" Tehran called out.

"Yes, our first class is tomorrow, Dad!" Whip said. "Bye!"

"You just skipped breakfast!" said Tehran.

"Don't worry! We'll pick up some food on the way!" Whip called back. "Love you, miss you, see you Christmas or so, BYE!!" Bobi drove the van out of the neighborhood. Tehran watched the boys go.

"So long, my son," he said. "Hope you do good." He went back in his house. As he did, his daughter approached him.

"Where has Whip gone?" she asked.

"He's gone off to college for a special thing," said Tehran.

"College? Wow," Sarah said.

"When you grow up with plenty of education," said Corbin from the table, "you'll find something to do there."

"Whip will be there for the next three years," said Tehran.

"Three years??" Sarah said in astonishment. "I can't wait that long." She walked into the living room.

"You'll wait a long time until it's your turn," said Corbin.

Sarah sat on the living room couch next to her stuffed dragon.

"Fredwick," she started talking. "My brother's going to college and tomorrow's my first day of third grade."

"You'll someday grow up," said Fredwick, "you'll get used to the real world and forget about me."

"That's a lot a shame," said Sarah.

Tehran walked up the stairs and looked into his son's bedroom. Posters were taken off the walls. The room looked very clean. Tehran found the antique typewriter on the homework desk in the corner. It had some paper in it. Tehran walked to it. He moved his hand with three fingers over its keyboard.

"Whip," he whispered to himself. Tears came to his eyes. He wiped them and looked into Whip's dresser mirror. He was about to miss his son.

And so, out on the open highway, Whip, Bobi, Pition, and their latest pal, Fentruck, made their way through the northwestern section of Virginia, heading for Harrisonburg. Whip held the map. Pition used his tail to point their location on the road.

"Okay, dudes, um south, er—east," he said. "Hold on I'm lost here. I'm like Christopher Columbus."

"Don't worry, Pition," said Whip, "Columbus was a fine man who took care of himself."

"That's what I believed," said Fentruck, "although he was a famous failure."

Bobi stopped the van in an intersection and went to the right.

"Wait a minute, I'm confused," said Pition looking at the map again. "That's the other Nefer and Qaba."

"Qaba-Quack and Nefer, what are you talking about here?" Whip asked.

"No," said Bobi leaning from the steering wheel on the map. "It's right there in the middle." He pointed to Appomattox.

"Yeah, Pition, Bobi's right," said Whip. The guys all stared at the map as Bobi wiggled the van side to side. He later stopped wiggling and drove straight.

"Um, hey, Bobe," said Whip.

"Yeah," said Bobi.

"Who's driving?" Whip asked.

The guys all looked through the windshield. Outside was a business truck about to collide with them. The boys shrieked and waved around in danger. Bobi quickly drove the van out of the truck's way. They were on the wrong side of road. Bobi drove into a cornfield nearby. They all rode through it and knocked away the stalks. They also ran into a scarecrow.

"Whoa! Scarecrow!" said Bobi.

"Forget 'scare crow', it's scaring the citizens here," said Pition.

Bobi moved the van through the field and finally ended up on a side road by a large educational center built of bricks far ahead through many lawns of grass. Whip read the sign: "Appalachian University, Harrisonburg. We made it, guys." Bobi drove the van into a driveway at the side of the grass lawn. The boys finally got into the university. People were walking around, unpacking their stuff from their vehicles.

"Check it OUT, man!" exclaimed Bobi. He drove slowly around each neighboring building. The university was surrounded by gangs, clubs, and bars. Suddenly, Bobi found something familiar as he drove by.

"Look," he said as he witnessed an igloo-like architectural building. "I spy the Arctic house. Which means..." he pointed to an arctic fox standing on the doorstep. "…that white fox character right there…is the one…the only…" The boys spoke together and said, "Angus Wellington, Jr."

"Whoa," said Pition. "The College Amusers King."

"King of the Amusers, huh?" said Fentruck.

"Just wait 'til he sees my moves," said Whip.

"Gee-whiz, yeah," said Bobi. "This is a sexy place to be."

"You've been saying that for the past two hours," said Pition. Bobi continued driving around, exploring the entire area.

CHAPTER 5

Tehran's Job Loss

Meanwhile, Tehran had a job at the office in a neighboring large city by Psyville. He had a meeting with his co-workers and boss, a rhinoceros. They explained about changes for Virginia. Tehran was speechless throughout the meeting. As it was done, the workers went back to their desks with bordering walls within. As Tehran looked at the pictures on his desk, memories came along when Whip was in some of them. There was a picture of 8-year-old Whip wearing a baseball uniform.

"Watch me swing the bat, Dad," Tehran imagined his son saying that.

Tehran sighed. Then he said, "Whip."

Later on, he worked on the computer. He researched some careers for the future of his son. He believed that Whip would be a philosopher like Socrates or Aristotle. Tehran researched the solar system and myths and folklores with Google®. He pictured a figure of his son's head. He imagined him saying, "Hi, Dad."

"My son," Tehran said.

Suddenly, a security camera looked at him. It was the office boss speaking, "Mr. Psy!" Tehran awoke when he heard the shouting voice. The boss continued, "Research programs are only for research consultants."

Tehran closed the internet.

"Stop this laziness," the boss said, "and get back to work! Or else…!!"

Tehran remembered an essay he had to type. He opened that document and suddenly somebody sneezed. Tehran's computer vibrated.

"Gesundheit," he said to the worker on the other side who sneezed. He worked on his essay. He got to the end of it. He clicked on the print button. The printer was busy with other workers' essays. Suddenly, it started to malfunction. It ran out of power. All of a sudden, the office's electricity blacked out in two seconds, the light on the ceiling and the computers. The workers got out and headed for the door. But Tehran stayed in the same place.

What have I done? He thought. Suddenly, the boss came in with his flashlight. Security guards followed him. The boss was angry. He snorted and his nose horn shone from an outside window. His eyes twitched. He found Tehran at his desk. The boss shone his flashlight on him.

"Mr. Tehran Psy!" he said. "I've warned you for the last time. Yoooouuu'rrrre..." he had his lips vibrate and then shouted "... FIIIIRRRRREEED!!" His uvula wiggled. The echo of his voice sounded through the room. The security guards took Tehran to the elevator and out of the building.

CHAPTER 6

The Moves, Part 1

And so, back in the university, Whip, Bobi, Pition, and Fentruck were performing stunts on sporting wheel sets. Whip rode his skateboard, Bobi rolled on his rollerblades, Pition had a set of wheels with boards tied on his thorax and tail base that allowed him to do tricks with his body as he rolled on them, like adjusting and stretching like a slinky, and Fentruck rode on a scooter that he packed on the way. Whip did a 360 flip trick and landed on the ground. The boys started singing "We've Got It Goin' On" by the Backstreet Boys.

Bobi opened his legs and performed a split kick in the air as he jumped. Pition wiggled his body as he rode on his wheel boards. He leaped into the air and performed a whiplash trick. Fentruck ran by a ramp. He ran over it and did a 540 spin trick in the air. The other boys ground on a stair rail down to a lower level. Then Fentruck landed with them. They continued singing. Whip found some guys lifting a couch and carrying it to their dorm. He rode on his skateboard and ducked under it as he moved.

The boys teamed up again as they sang the song's chorus.

They repeated the chorus. Suddenly, a Frisbee flew by Whip. He caught it. He spun it on his finger. The guys continued their riding mission.

"Nice move, Whip," said Bobi, "that was tight!" He chuckled.

Suddenly, they passed the Arctics' playground. Some were playing volleyball. Others sat on the front steps. A big horn sheep witnessed the guys' moves.

"Whoa," he said, he pointed his hoof at Whip and his pals. "Did you see that?"

The others turned around at the scene of rolling tricks.

"Well, well, well," said the polar bear Arctic member, "look what the new guys have got for their major, some new grade-A meat."

"Hey, hey, easy, big fella," said Angus Wellington, Jr., "that grade-A meat looks like Arctic style. Let's check them out." He turned back to his teammates and pointed his thumb at the igloo-like building. "Arctics, we're off!" They all dashed into the building, got changed and got their skateboards, scooters, and rollerblades to go out and follow Whip.

Meanwhile, Whip tossed the Frisbee in his hand to a guy that jumped and caught the Frisbee in his mouth. He landed on the ground and raised his hand. After that, the boys stopped for a little bit of a reason.

"Check it out," said Pition pointing his tail behind himself and the others. "Look who's following us."

A guy was carrying books across the road, but Angus Wellington, Jr. and his Arctics got passed him and knocked him down. They continued to follow the heroes.

"Ha ha," Whip laughed. "Let's just make sure it stays that way." They guys continued their journey. The Arctics kept following them. The guys ended singing.

"Bump!" said Bobi as he ended the song. They all stopped riding on their wheel sets. They ended up by a bar called "A Petit Fraîche".

"Well, guys," said Whip, "we're gonna be the greatest creatures for the rest of our lives." The crew walked into the bar. They walked down the entrance stairs. There was barely any light. People consumed coffee and churros.

"You guys grab a table and I'll grab the goodies," Whip told his friends. Whip went to the serving counter to buy some refreshments. The others looked for an empty table. The Arctics entered the bar.

There was a French girl talking in the microphone in her language. Bobi claimed to remember taking French back in high school. As Whip waited for his order at the counter, he listened to the French speech. Whip used his powerful mind to translate the language and read it in English. The speech was a poem of nature and beauty. And so, as it was over, the people clapped their hands. The curtain rolled over closing and opening the stage. The French girl bowed.

"Bravo! Encore!" shouted Bobi. "That was enchanting!" He fainted from his chair to the floor.

CHAPTER 7

Meet the Arctics

"Check it out, Angus," said the Arctic polar bear member, "he's over there." He pointed to Whip who was paying for the refreshments in the bar. He got a tray with soda bottles and beef jerky. Angus Wellington, Jr. gave his helmet in the polar bear's paw.

"I'm going to give him an Arctic welcome," he said. He walked to Whip. Whip carried the tray from the counter as Angus bumped into him. One of the bottles fell down. Angus jumped back.

"Oops!" he said. "I'll get that." He picked up the bottle and gave it back to Whip.

"Thanks," said Whip. "Sorry about that, I didn't…"

"No no," said Angus. "It's fine, it's all right. I just wanted to introduce myself to you."

"Well, good," said Whip putting the tray back on the counter. "Social interaction is a necessary thing. In fact, genius is my best part of sensuality. Hi, my name is Whip." He put up his hand showing it to Angus. "Whip Psy."

"Angus." He introduced himself. "Angus Wellington, Jr."

The polar bear chuckled.

"Oh yes and my right hand man," said Angus, "Tubbs the Polar Bear."

The polar bear chuckled again and said, "The pleasure's all mine, dude." He zoomed his head closer down to Whip and Angus. "Welcome aboard the Arctic Express. The big kind." He rose himself back up.

"Whip," said Angus. "We are the number 10 team of the College Amusers and we've won every competition since the beginning. And we were deciding to make you…" He pointed his front digits at Whip. "… our first draft pick. Lucky you, huh, what do you think of that?"

"Well, I'm not an arctic animal," said Whip. "But I have a walrus pal with me. But not a chance, though. You want us to be Arctics?" He turned to his friends and laughed. "Hey, guys, did you hear that? We're gonna be part of the…"

"Hold on, I think you misunderstood," Angus interrupted. "This reservation's only for one individual." He showed one digit.

"Oh," said Whip, "well I'm sorry but, you see? Pition, Bobi, Fentruck and I are in this together. It's all of us…or none but me."

"Whip, Whip. You don't want to be laid down by those clowns, do you? I thought you wanted to win."

Whip chuckled and said, "That's just what we're going to do. They're the real geniuses as my teammates. They've been friends of mine since high school. Now we're serious athletes."

Meanwhile, Bobi got cork plugs for beverage bottles and stuck them in his nostrils. He turned around to the others and said, "Check this out, man!"

The Arctics laughed and laughed. Tubbs the polar bear said, "The only contest you could ever win is the 'idiot' contest." He kept laughing with his teammates. Angus snapped his digits. The Arctics stopped and stood left face like soldiers.

"Whoa, cool trick," said Bobi. "Watch this." He slammed a fist on his head and blew the cork plugs out of his nostrils. He caught them in his palm. "Ta da."

"Nice," said the Arctic puffin.

"Cool magic trick," said the big horn sheep. Those animals turned back with their team.

"Man, Angus," said Bobi, "do these guys go fetch and play dead, too?"

"Why, yes," said Angus. "As a matter of fact they do." "Arctics," he commanded. "Play fetch!"

"Uh oh," said Bobi. He slowly moved back as the Arctics approached him. "This is not good at all."

Tubbs snatched a biting strike. Fentruck got a stick that he used for a weapon.

"Back off, you Arctic fiends!" he said. "I've got a Bo staff and I'm not afraid to use it!" He swished it like a teacher's pointing rod. Then he grasped both of his flippers on each end and did a ninja stick battle move with it.

"Whoa!" said the Arctics as they jumped back altogether.

"Alright, that's enough!" Angus said aloud. "No more fighting." He turned to Whip and said, "I thought we were friends. I heard about your vacation and you met the white tigers, the Satvrinskis. 'Cause I knew Prince Aborabor. He and I were friends before then. Perhaps we'll all meet together at the Arctic Igloo fraternity."

"Igloo?" said Pition. "Who would ever want to join a camp of Eskimos by the fire?"

"Tubbs," Angus said to that polar bear who turned to him.

"Now let's see here," Tubbs picked up Pition. He clutched one paw gently on his neck and the other paw slowly slid down Pition's body length.

"D-Don't choke me!" said Pition. "Watch my scales!"

"I'm just feeling how scaly you are, Mr. Snake," said Tubbs.

"Please try not to stretch me out," Pition said panicking. Tubbs's paw reached the base of Pition's tail.

"Hey, leave him alone!" Whip shouted as he charged toward Tubbs. Other Arctics blocked his path. Whip shoved himself between an elephant seal and a puffin. "Bobi!" he shouted. The big horn sheep held Bobi by his tail and feet.

"Don't worry, pal!" Bobi said to Whip. "I'm a significant reptile." He spread his digits of his front foot and stabbed them on the sheep's leg. The big horn sheep bleated in pain and dropped Bobi on the floor. He got up. "All right, you Evil Knievel!" he shouted as he confronted Angus. "You lay off of my genius friend!" The Arctics backed away from Whip. Suddenly, a light switched on as bright as a star.

"Hey!" the French girl on stage shouted as she started speaking English. "Boys." The guys all blocked the light from their eyes. The French girl continued speaking, "Let's stop loafing around here, shall we? I've got business that you are interrupting. It's for my performance..." she walked toward the Arctics. "...of my ingenious passion in this bar."

"Ooh, passion, eh?" Angus giggled. "You've got quite a style here, mademoiselle. Anyway, I'm busy right now."

"Well, I'm really pissed about all this mess you're making in my bar," said the French girl.

"I surely have the reality of human intelligence like yours distracting me here," said Angus.

"Ha!" the French girl snapped her fingers in front of Angus. A musician tapped his drums by the stage. The French girl confronted Angus and said, "You surely knock me away, Mr. Fox. You are the intruder of a famous French bar of mine from every…" She started raising her voice. "…direction of an enemy on my rear!" She snapped her fingers in front of Angus again. Suddenly music started playing with momentary beats. The people in the bar snapped their fingers repeatedly second by second. The gangster musician played his drum and started singing, "Get…out…of…here,…fool…yeah." The finger snaps and music went on and on.

A while passed. Angus suddenly got angry and was about to throw a tantrum. He growled and shouted, "ALRIGHT! THAT'S ENOUGH!" The snapping and music stopped.

"What's wrong, A.J.?" asked Whip. "Not as well as a real Wellington, are you?"

"Don't you DARE talk to me that way!" Angus scolded putting up a digit in anger.

"Yeah," said Tubbs next to him. "Don't forget, he's the king, little punk."

Whip giggled and said, "Well, we'll dethrone you AND your Arctic friends, your royal lowness. You'd be lucky to be my engine assistant."

"Then we will see who wins or loses," said Angus as he put up his paw. "Is that a deal?"

"You've got a deal," said Whip as he shook Angus's paw.

"And be sure to wipe the dirt from my shoes…Freshman geniuses. Arctics OUT!" Angus led the Arctics out of the bar. Whip and his friends remained.

Suddenly, a human guy decorated with tattoos and nearly bald approached the heroes.

"Hey," he said. Whip and his friends turned to him. The guy continued, "That French girl is the boss of this bar. So you all need to be careful about her."

"Okay," said Whip. "Who are you?"

"Name's Gaston Sexton," said the guy.

"No way," said Bobi. "That's the name of the bad guy from Disney's *Beauty and the Beast.*"

"My parents didn't know what name to give me when I was a kid," said Gaston Sexton. "So I came up with that name myself. It used to be Gus."

"That's unusual," said Whip.

"I have two younger brothers named, Jason and Kyle," said Gaston. "I have a club if you want to visit. It's called 'The Shoe Gone Quazy Club'."

"That's like saying 'sure gone crazy'," said Pition.

"Right," said Gaston. "There is also a dance this Saturday along with a custom-made concert with karaoke."

"Oh, sick," said Bobi. "We're interested."

"I'm not good at dancing the real way," said Pition. "I make my own moves."

"So do I," said Bobi.

"That means we get to pick a song to sing," said Whip.

"Catch you guys later, I gotta go," said Gaston. "And whatever you are…" he said to Whip, "…be sexy." He exited the bar up the stairs.

"Here we go," said Whip. He and his pals went out of the bar.

CHAPTER 8

Back to College for Tehran

And so, after Tehran was fired, he went to an office by the educational center in Harrisonburg where his son was accepted. In that office, a worker went out of a secretary's office.

"Next," said the voice of another secretary.

Tehran went into an office and sat in a chair in front of a fat blue owl's desk. The blue name stand read "Mrs. Prunella Woods". This owl secretary looked at a paper about Tehran's education and classes that were taken.

"Well, Mr. Tehran Psy," she said, "I have noticed you don't have a college degree."

"Well," said Tehran, "I did complete three years of it."

"Look, sir," said Mrs. Woods, "I'm afraid we've gone in reverse for other people to get their college degrees." She flew with the paper in her foot and set it in a cabinet's top drawer. "So, what do you need?"

"We're talking about…" said Tehran, "…a degree?"

"Yes sir, we have a real winner of every sort!" Mrs. Woods exclaimed.

Tehran lowered his head and sighed. "What's a psyvark to do?"

Mrs. Woods flew by him and said, "Look here now, Mr. Psy. The reality about an educational degree is simple. Plus it *is* everything. And the only way to build another career is to go back to college."

"College?!?" said Tehran. "Me?? Well, I was there during the early '70s. I'm quite too old for that now."

"Come on, sir," said Mrs. Woods, "you're never too old to learn a new trick."

Tehran gave one last stare at the idea. He agreed with the secretary.

CHAPTER 9

The Regular Classes

And so, the boys were finally in their regular classes. Majors were not yet decided. Whip, Bobi, Pition, and Fentruck participated in an American Government classroom. The professor made announcements with the principles of government. As he made his theory about it, Tubbs had made a spit gun out of a straw. He sat behind the heroes and wadded a straw wrapper and spat it through the straw at Whip's head. Whip turned around as he was distracted. He saw the Arctics sitting behind him and his friends. Tubbs giggled deeply. The professor continued speaking. Tubbs created another spit wad and shot it at Bobi.

"Ah," Bobi said as he felt the wad on the back of his head. "Mother, I didn't do it."

The professor was still in the middle of his speech with the textbook on his desk. Suddenly, the door opened.

"Hello," it was Tehran. "Excuse me for interrupting," he said to the professor, "I've been sent back here to college and…"

"Go ahead," said the professor. "Have a seat."

Tehran walked around to find a seat. He found his son. He softly said, "Hello, Whip."

Whip jumped and shouted in surprise. "Dad," he said.

"Dude," said a student in front of Whip, turning back to him. "You're disrupting the class."

"Sorry," said Whip.

"Um…" said Tehran clearing his throat, "I'm his father." The other students were astonished when they listened. They all started laughing together.

"Students, students!" the professor called out. "This is a constant disruption!"

The students kept laughing. The Arctics made fun of the situation.

"Daddy's little kid couldn't be alone?" said Angus.

Whip felt an insult. He whimpered and suddenly screamed, "NOOOOOOOOO!!!" The nightmare went on and on.

CHAPTER 10

Father and Son Together Again

After all the laughter, Whip went with his father and got some textbooks. Tehran told his story to his son: "I got fired from the office, so I am back here at college to get a degree."

"Well, I'm sorry to hear about that, Dad," said Whip.

"But fear not," said Tehran. "I will get that degree on the double." As he carried his textbooks to a nearby bench, he slipped on a cylinder-shaped flask from an empty soda drunk by another person who was there before. Tehran caught himself on the bench. His textbooks fell on the cement ground. Whip set his books on a nearby planter wall. He helped his father pick up the other books.

"Dad," he said. "What I was saying is that you're disrupting my classes."

"Don't be ashamed," said Tehran. "Things make me perfectly formal."

"First idea," said Whip. "Please don't interrupt my classes like that."

"I'm not trying to interrupt things; I just wanted to find you around here."

"Dad," Whip put his hand on his father's forehead. "You're scaring people." He moved his hand away.

"Nothing to be ashamed of," said Tehran. "Two psyvarks are better than one."

"Two psyvarks, alright," said Whip.

"I'm afraid you're going to be stuck with me for this first year in college," said Tehran.

"Right."

Tehran hugged Whip. "It's another year with you and me."

"So what happened, Dad?"

"I got fired from the office, that's all."

CHAPTER 11

The Mystic Four

Skimming to the evening, Whip, Bobi, Pition, and Fentruck were in their dormitory room. They had bunk beds and a desk with a computer for online services in the university. As the boys had a discussion about Whip's father being with him the same year, Pition exclaimed, "A year?!?" He slithered on the floor carpet and babbled, "He didn't say a year, did he?"

"Yes," said Whip. "He did."

"Dude," said Bobi in one of the beds. "A year is like a pretty long time."

"That's twelve months, Bobe," said Whip.

"So you're stuck with your father this year, aren't you, Whip," said Fentruck.

"Yeah," Whip said. "He was fired and he can't get a real job."

"Fired? Wow," said Bobi. "That's a shame. But at least he's got the power like you, right?"

"Pretty much," said Whip.

The boys stayed silent for a few minutes. Then Whip came up with an ingenious idea.

"I've got it!" he shouted. "Let's make ourselves superheroes. We are known as the 'Mystic Four'. Remember the Marvel Comics 'The Fantastic Four'."

"Oh, yeah," said Bobi. "The Thing, Mr. Fantastic, the Human Torch, and the Invisible Woman."

"Exactly," said Whip. "I'll call myself the Mythical Creature, Bobi, you are um…" He thought of other names for a minute. "…the Croc-O-Dial, like dialing a telephone number."

"Whoa, great name," said Bobi.

"Pition will be known as Mr. Constrictor," said Whip, "and Fentruck can be 'The Walrus'."

Pition nodded his head.

"How boring," said Fentruck. "But it's fine at least."

"And I believe," said Whip, "our nemesis will be called 'Dr. Cheater' if those Arctics ever cheat around us."

"Right," said Bobi. "That Angus Wellington, Jr. might always win by cheating at those historical competitions."

The boys used their imaginations with their superhero names.

The following is in comics:

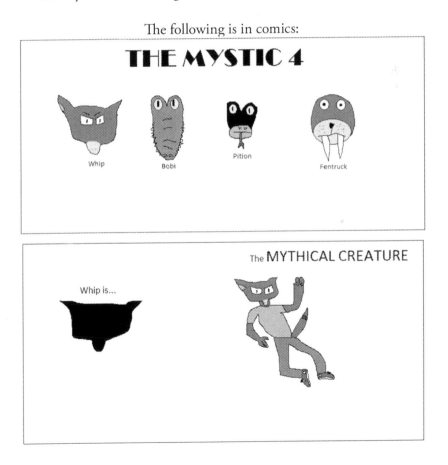

The boys ended their imagination.

"Okay, guys," said Whip. "We're all set on that idea."

"Oh yeah, guys!" Bobi called up to explain something. "There is this video I downloaded on my computer at home. It's a music video of a band called the 'Rapping Dipers', which is like saying 'wrapping diapers'. And they're singing 'Joy is ours and we'll never lose it/Never even think to ever compose it/Yeah…' and so on. This kid, who is the lead singer, is actually white but he sings with a black accent. It's got kids rapping in it. I don't know where it comes from."

"Great," said Whip. "Now let me explain the ground rules. No pretending that things are what we imagine, no spreading announcements in public, and no acting like relatives. 'Cause we've got our own that are our unique species. They've got their lives. We've got *our* lives." An echo of "Our lives" bounced through a vent on the ceiling repeating again.

"Spooky," said Bobi. He tried sleeping.

Fentruck remembered his old home with the oysters and his partner, Crow Buck (a crow). His memories went on and on. He frowned and his eyes nearly closed. Pition slithered by him.

"You don't look too good, Fenny," he said, "are you all right?"

"I'll be fine," said Fentruck. "I just need some water from the fountain." He suddenly fell over Pition. Pition screamed as Fentruck squished him.

"Fnntrk," Pition said as Fentruck was on him. He used his tail to tap his side. Fentruck got up and walked into the hallway to get a drink from a nearby fountain. Then he went back to the room and all the boys went to bed.

CHAPTER 12

The Next Day

The next day arrived. Someone jogged from his house down the road by the university. In the boys' dorm, they slept for the early morning by seven. Someone knocked on the door and opened it.

"Good morning, boys," it was Tehran. "Rise and shine. School is about to come."

Whip snored and woke up barely opening his eyes as the others snored about to get up from bed.

"Dad," said Whip. "Our first class is not till noon."

"Well, I just wanted to make sure…" Tehran stepped by the bunk beds and slipped on Whip's skateboard and rolled toward the window. He pulled on the string to lift the shading straps up and the outside light lit the dark room. The light was too bright so the boys panicked. Tehran got from the floor from his accident. The boys frowned at each other. Tehran hummed.

Later in the morning before the first periods, Tehran paid for the boys' lunch in the cafeteria.

Whip, Bobi, Pition, and Fentruck participated in their first period classrooms separately. Some had English classes and science with biology and technology. With their knowledge they were able to accomplish homework between other classes.

After the classes into the evening, the boys would go to the bars by the university and play pool with gangsters. Thus Whip, Bobi, Pition, and Fentruck don't drink alcohol.

After evening break, the boys would get fast food and somewhat finish homework, sometimes using tape recorders for notes to take.

In the days going by, Angus let a young deer doe sit by him and his Arctic partners. So he made room by moving his puffin partner down the seat row toward Tubbs. The doe sat down with Angus.

CHAPTER 13

Spare Time in the Library

It became Friday of the first week in college. The boys came into the library and so did Tehran. They all went forward to get library cards so they could check out a reading book.

"Sign here," said the librarian as he showed them a clipboard with bars of names signed. Whip used the pen held on a string to sign in, then Bobi, then Fentruck, then Pition, and Tehran. They all went to check out books to read for any empty time. As Tehran took a seat at a table nearby, the boys toured around and saw paintings on the walls of classic television series of the previous decade.

"Cool beans!" said Whip. "The 'Teenage Mutant Ninja Turtles™', and the 'Mighty Morphin' Power Rangers™', they're painted on an old wall in a big city here."

"Look over here," said Bobi. "The 'Street Sharks™', man I miss that show."

"I see posters of 'Pokémon™'," said Pition.

"Whoever was last here must have had permission to decorate this place," said Whip.

"And on the ceiling there is…" said Fentruck, "…Earthworm Jim, Sonic the Hedgehog, Spyro the Dragon, and Crash Bandicoot."

"I can't believe how cool they made this library in college," said Bobi. "I'm gonna read a book." He sat at a table to read a novel that he checked out. Then so did Whip and Pition. Fentruck warmed up an early lunch of popcorn shrimp, borrowing a microwave oven. He walked to the others.

"I'm gonna have my brunch of shrimp in the cafeteria," he said. "I'll meet you guys later."

"Alright," said Whip and Bobi simultaneously.

Fentruck went to the cafeteria. Suddenly, more customers came by.

CHAPTER 14

Draco Malfunction

"Hey, guys," said a white mouse passing by, carrying a box.

"Hey, Steven," said Bobi as he kept reading.

"You know him?" asked Whip.

"Yeah," said Bobi. "He's in my biology class this year."

"Oh yeah, I've seen him around a few times," said Pition.

"That's Steven Simmons," said Bobi. "He's a cool guy." The boys went up to meet Steven Simmons.

"What's in that box?" asked Whip.

"My cool robot," Steven said as he opened the box. It was a man-like robot with flat feet.

"Wow, that looks like *The Iron Giant,*" said Bobi.

"You know Hogarth Hughes, Kent Mansley…?" said Whip.

"Yeah, I love that movie," said Steven.

"Me, too," said a human guy in the back, reading an encyclopedia. He appeared with a small, round nose and a black medieval hair style. The boys turned to him.

"The name's Landon," said the guy, "Landon Baines. Other guys call me 'Pageboy', 'cause I have this medieval haircut."

"Actually, you look great," said Whip.

"Totally cool," Bobi added.

"Want to see my invention?" said Landon as he lifted his backpack on the table. He got out what looked like a rubber toy dragon. "This is a recorder. It may look like a dragon, but it talks with a recorded tape inside its belly." He opened the belly to show an opening flap with a small tape. "See?"

"We see," said Whip, Bobi, and Pition simultaneously.

Landon turned on his dragon tape recorder and it said notes through the mouth. Landon took the notes and wrote them on a sheet of lined paper.

"Impressive," said Whip.

Suddenly, Fentruck had finished his shrimp lunch and returned to the library. He rejoined the guys.

"Am I late? What did I miss?" he asked.

"We're looking at some guys' inventions here," said Whip.

The dragon started to mess up its quote by ruining the tape.

"Oh no!" said Landon as he quickly grabbed it and pressed the stop button. "I've got a malfunctioning dragon here." He took a look inside the tape recorder. The tape's line was caught in a tiny rod. He grabbed it and swept it off.

"Draco Malfunction," said Bobi.

"There is a problem with this tape," said Landon.

"Draco Malfunction?" Whip asked Bobi.

"Yeah," said Bobi, "like Draco Malfoy from the *Harry Potter* books. 'Cause 'Draco' means 'dragon', so this mechanical dragon is broken…"

"I see, I get it," said Whip.

"That's pretty neat, though," said Fentruck.

"It's time for a superhero performance!" Steven called Landon. Landon followed him to a nearby closet next to the bookshelves.

CHAPTER 15

Ratman and Bobbin

Steven and Landon changed into suits to show their secret identities to the main guys.

"We're Ratman and Bobbin," said Steven and Landon. Steven was dressed in a black suit with a blue cape and a yellow eye mask. Landon was dressed in a red suit with a roll of rope around his waist, along with a green eye mask.

"It's like Batman and Robin only you switch the first letters of each name," said Landon.

"Cool," said Bobi.

"Double cool," said Pition.

Suddenly, some mosquitoes buzzed inside through the windows.

"Uh oh," said Steven. "We've got bugs to kill. Get the swatters!"

"Right away," said Landon. Those boys grabbed fly swatters from nails on a nearby wall between bookcases. They started swatting mosquitoes one by one. A mosquito hawk entered the scene.

"Holy fart knockers!" said Landon. "A mosquito hawk!"

"Quick, Bobbin!" said Steven. "Swatters up!" They both swatted and swatted until the bug was dead.

"Come on," said Pition to Whip. "We're supposed to be practicing for the Amusers."

"The library is saved," said Steven and Landon.

"Come on, guys, we're out of here," said Whip as he and his friends went out through an exit out of the library.

"Boys!" the librarian called to Steven and Landon. "What are you doing to my library?"

"Um," said Steven, "we're just making it neat and keeping it clean."

"Well, don't mess with anything," said the librarian.

"Yes, sir," said Landon, saluting.

The librarian continued working on his computer. Tehran got up from reading a large book when he had heard Whip and the others leave the library. He went to the exit to follow their steps outdoors.

"Whip!" he said. "Boys!"

CHAPTER 16

The Moves, Part 2

The boys were practicing stunts within the field of trees. Bobi exercised by climbing a tree. Whip skated on a metal half pipe in the middle of the field. He did amazing flip tricks and grab tricks. Pition dug holes in the ground and maneuvered through the soil. Fentruck used a mallet to hammer a peg by a tree. As they all practiced their moves, Tehran found them around a crowd in the woods.

"Where's my son?" he asked himself. Whip skated on the wall in front of him. "There he is!" Tehran said. "Whip!" he called to him. Whip was distracted as he ground on a rail and stopped. He fell off his skateboard and landed on his hands and knees. Luckily, he wore a helmet and pads on his elbows and knees.

"Yes, Dad!" he called back as he got up and grabbed his board. He climbed out of the skating pit up to his father.

"I have something to tell you, son," Tehran said. "There are many legends in a book that say that genius goes beyond our world."

"I get that, Dad," said Whip. "That's still a myth." He set his board down.

"It *is* a myth," said Tehran, stepping by him. "But someday you'll get used to it. WHOA!" He accidentally stepped on Whip's skateboard and slid down into the pit. He started riding it everywhere he went. He tried performing some of Whip's tricks of grinding, flipping, and grabbing the board. Suddenly, the Arctics arrived at the scene. They found Tehran skating in the pit.

"Hey, that guy is good at skating," said the Arctic snowy owl.

"Yeah, but that's not our right person," said Angus.

Tehran suddenly ended up at a high ramp. He was launched high into the air above the trees. He fell back down. As he did, he used a magical force to slow him down like a parachute. Then he gently landed back in the pit. He walked by the Arctics, tossed Whip's skateboard back up the ledge and climbed out back onto the grass. Whip grabbed his skateboard and helped his father up.

"I can't believe I was able to fly like that," said Tehran. "Hey, son, what if I join your team. We can practice together and we'll both have fun."

Whip took off his helmet and said, "Dad, it *is* fun as it sounds. But there are no openings..." he spread out his hand in front of his father. "... on my team. Okay?" He walked away to rejoin his friends by the trees.

Just then, Angus confronted Tehran and said, "Mr. Psy. I've never seen such a man your age do those moves like your son."

"Well, thanks," said Tehran, "whoever you gentlemen are."

"The uh,...Arctics," said Angus, "team number 10 of the history of the Amusers. We have a special opening on *our* team. It's got your name on it, sir..." he patted Tehran's side. "...be a winner." The other Arctics surrounded Tehran. They all laughed.

"H-hey!" said Tubbs the polar bear. "Welcome to the team, mister."

"Do you think that's a good idea, Whip?" asked Bobi.

"I don't know," said Whip. "But I guess we'll try something."

"Thanks, gentlemen," said Tehran to the Arctics. "But I'm only interested in staying close to my son."

Angus sighed. "I'm not sure you would understand this one simple life time opportunity with us away from your family."

"I don't suppose you understand the true relationship of a father and son together," said Tehran.

"Guys," Whip said to his friends, "I have a plan."

"Well if you change your mind," said Angus to Tehran, "here's my card for the team." He handed him a card with an invitation to the Arctics' igloo. "Arctics, let's pack it up." All the Arctics left as Tehran moved a bit as he looked at the invitation. Whip suddenly approached him.

"Listen, Dad," he said, "next to our team, the Arctics have an opening on theirs."

"Oh yeah, hi, Mr. Psy," said Pition. "The Arctics are way off the top cool."

"I'll take the idea," said Tehran. He ran back to the Arctics as they were about to leave.

"Hey!" Tehran called to them. "Mr. Wellington, I suppose!"

"Yes, that's my name," said Angus.

"You can count me in," said Tehran.

"All right then," said the Arctics. Angus put up a pinning plate that said "Arctic".

"Arctic brother Tehran," he said "let me present you with your Arctic pledge pin." He poked the pin's needle into the breast pocket of Tehran's button shirt. "Arctics!" Angus said. "Exit." The Arctics left the field as Tehran stared at his new pin.

"Tehran!" Angus called him. Tehran followed the Arctics.

"Wow! Way to go, Whip!" shouted Bobi.

"Hoo hoo, yeah baby!" said Pition.

CHAPTER 17

The Shoe Gone Quazy Club

And so, Whip and his pals were invited to the home of the Sexton family. They spoke with Mr. Sexton about his sons: Gaston, Jason, and Kyle. Those guys invited the heroes to their club, the Shoe Gone Quazy Club.

"So my son sent for you guys, eh?" asked Mr. Sexton.

"Yes, sir," said Whip. "He gives us advice on social interaction."

"Yeah," said Bobi, "he says 'Hey, be sexy' and stuff."

"Did I tell somebody to take out this trash?!" shouted Mrs. Sexton inside the house.

"I'll do it in a minute!" Mr. Sexton called to her. "I'm talking to somebody here!" He turned back to the boys. "Gaston moved away some time ago with some friends he's living with." He got up from his chair and said, "But keep in mind, there are drugs those guys are addicted to."

"We'll make a notice, sir," said Whip. Suddenly, Gaston drove a truck to pick up the main boys.

"Come have a ride in my sexy Chevy!" he called to them honking the horn. The three boys went to him and climbed into the Chevy truck.

"How are y'all doing?" Gaston asked.

"We're cool," said Bobi.

"Ready for my club?" asked Gaston.

"We are all hip," said Whip and Pition simultaneously.

Gaston drove the boys to the house of his club. The sign at the top said "Shoe Gone Quazy Club". They were at the right place. They walked out of the truck and inside the clubhouse. It had brown wood covering it and two floors. The guys walked in and settled on couches in the middle of the first floor's lounge.

"Man, this *is* the perfect place to be sexy," said Bobi.

"Indeed," said Gaston.

"How about a song?" asked Pition.

"Good idea," said Gaston. "I'll get everyone's attention." He called out to all the other club members. "Hey, everyone!" Everybody heard his shouting voice. They all came together into the lounge and beyond. "We are about to hear a song from our new guests!" Gaston announced.

And so Pition started singing: (A parody version of the Gaston song from Disney's *Beauty and the Beast*)

"Noooooo ooooooooone's slick as Gaston, No one's hip as Gaston
And nobody dares to play a trick on Gaston."

Gaston started singing as he moved by the club's indoor skate ramp:

"As a sexy man I feel perfect…"

He picked up his six-inch-wide skateboard.

"…Especially when I've got my board."

He started climbing up the wall to the top and began skating. He continued singing:

"My skills are tough in hardware
And it's all…in…my…hooooooooaaard!"

Whip, Bobi, Pition, and Fentruck sang another verse:

"Noooooooo ooooooooone skates like Gaston, No one's great as Gaston."

A raccoon in the club sang:

"And we all give a big piece of cake to Gaston."

Other boys sang:

"Well we can't afford to give him a head start
For we don't know if he has addictions.
Somebody can give him advice for any con…di…tioooooooooons."

Everybody in the club sang together, including the heroes:

"Noooooooo ooooooooone makes thrills like
Gaston, nor has skills like Gaston."

A raccoon by the kitchen sang:

"And nobody jumps over big hills like Gaston."

Gaston stopped skating. He went off the ramp and sang:

"Thank you all, gentlemen, I'm a genius
For if I have to go my way.
There's never anything left for anyone…to…saaaaaaaay!"

He went back to the couches with the heroes. Bobi and Pition sang another verse:

"Noooooooo oooooooone farts like Gaston, No one's smart as Gaston."

A skunk in the club sang:

"No one even throws so fast darts like Gaston."

Gaston said, "Thank you all just keep on singing."

The heroes sang one last verse:

"Nooooooo oooooooone thinks like Gaston, No one drinks like Gaston."

The raccoon in the club sang near the kitchen sink:

"Don't you ever put stuff in the sink, eh, Gaston?"

The skunk sang:

"At least he never stinks he's all clean."

Whip sang:

"We don't even know what he's on."

Bobi sang:

"His name what we call G-A-S…" He slowed down as he spelled Gaston's name. *"…T-O-N.* Everybody ready?" he asked the others.

Together they all shouted, *"GAAAASSSSTOOOOOOOOOOOOOOO OOOOOOO-OOOOOOOON!"* They ended the song.

CHAPTER 18

The Saturday Night Dance

After Whip, Bobi, Pition, and Fentruck left the club, they went to an old church hall where a big dance was run. The disc jockey played the song "Whip It" by Devo. People were dancing as the song went on.

"I think this should be our club's anthem," said Bobi.

"I think you're right," said Whip. "It's perfect."

"At least it has your name in it," said Bobi.

"I love the way your brain works, Bobe," said Pition as they all kept dancing back and forth.

The disc jockey changed the song to "Larger Than Life" by the Backstreet Boys. The boys imitated the music and the starting part going, "Yeeaaahhhh, ha ha ha haaaaa." The song went on.

The heroes started to create dance moves as the song went on.

Whip: Psyvark Step-Up

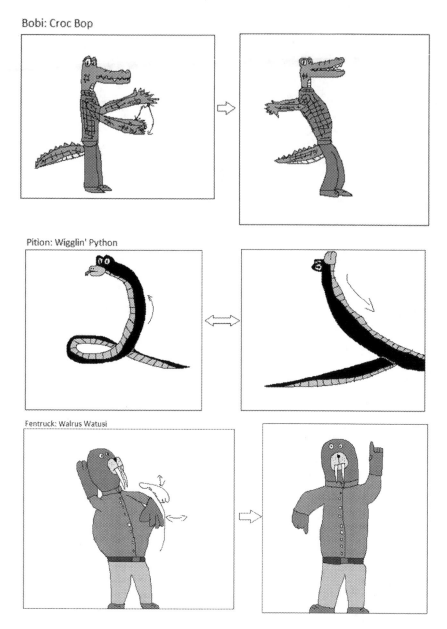

Bobi: Croc Bop

Pition: Wigglin' Python

Fentruck: Walrus Watusi

The song continued on as the boys kept dancing. Suddenly, an old cat came up to them and said, "You boys do such pretty well dances. I saw my nephew one time do a different kind of dance. I can hardly remember that."

"Thanks, sir," said Whip. "We're professionals plus geniuses."

"So I see," said the old cat as he walked away. Tehran walked into the gym.

"Boys!" he called out.

"Dad?" said Whip as he barely heard his father's voice the loud music.

"Mr. Psy!" cried the others as they followed Whip toward Tehran.

"There are tables coming in," said Tehran.

"Yeah, I saw them earlier," said Whip.

"They've got a bunch of chairs, too," said Bobi.

People brought all the tables and chairs into the gym.

"I'm going to get some food," said Bobi, "I haven't eaten since breakfast." He went into the gym's hall and looked for the kitchen. Whip, Pition, and Fentruck grabbed a table.

Suddenly, Gaston showed up on stage by the disc jockey and started speaking an announcement in the microphone.

CHAPTER 19

The Karaoke Concert

"Alright, people, attention please!" Gaston spoke out. "We're about to have something special here on stage. We have singers on this list..." He held a piece of paper with numbers and names. "...in numerical order of whom I will call on to come forward and sing his or her chosen song."

"How exciting is this, guys?" Whip asked his friends.

"I've got us a song," said Bobi. "We're singing "Bye Bye Bye" by *NSYNC."

Gaston continued his announcement: "First off, we will start with our famous French girl, Miss Beau Fraîche, with the song 'Material Girl' by Madonna."

Beau Fraîche is the girl's stage name. She seemed to have adopted a few words of her culture. Gaston gave her the microphone as the disc jockey started playing the assigned song. The French girl followed the music as she was ready to sing. So then she did.

"This is trippy," said Whip. Bobi returned with a small pan of tri-tip beef. He set it on the table and sat in his chair as the French girl continued singing the next verse.

The disc jockey sang the bridge repeating the words, *"Living in a material world",* as Beau sang *"Material"* each time. Then the French girl sang alone the last verse.

She sang the chorus and the rest of the song. Bobi ate his last slice of tri-tip. Then he placed the tray at the tip of his jaws and dumped the juice into his mouth. The French girl ended the song. The audience cheered and clapped, including the main heroes. Gaston grabbed the microphone and made another announcement:

"Alright! Everybody cool? Our next singer is Mr. Big Brown Bear with 'I Am... I Said' by Neil Diamond." He gave the microphone to the bear wearing a red sweater, a pair of sun shades, and a pair of brown leather shoes. The disc jockey started the song as the bear followed along. He started singing the first verse and the chorus.

The bear kept shaking his bottom and then cleared his throat singing the next verse.

The bear shouted the end of the song.

The song was over. The crowd cheered by whistling and clapping their hands. The bear walked off the stage as Gaston grabbed the microphone for the next announcement.

"Wasn't that exciting, people?!" he started talking. "Okay, we've got things running smoothly, now. Next!"

Upon the stage came "Pageboy" Landon Baines, one of the guys Whip and his pals met at the library. He spoke in the microphone and said, "Today I'm going to sing 'Piano Man' by Billy Joel."

The disc jockey started playing that song on the radio. Landon followed the music using his fingers as a harmonica on the starting part. He started singing the song.

He used his finger harmonica again, and then sang the chorus:

He gently clutched the microphone and lowered his voice, singing the next verse.

"What a genius," said Whip silently in the crowd. Bobi sipped the last of his meat juice out of the tray as Landon kept singing.

Landon used his finger harmonica as the song ended. The crowd cheered.

"Bravo, Pageboy!" shouted Bobi as he clapped his hands.

Gaston grabbed the microphone for the next announcement, "Well, there doesn't seem to be anybody next on the list. But it's free."

Whip and his friends ran up to the stage. Whip grabbed the microphone from Gaston and said, "We'll have a turn to sing."

"As you wish," said Gaston. "What do you want to sing?"

"'Bye Bye Bye' by *NSYNC," said Whip.

The disc jockey searched on his machine and found the correct song. Then he played it. Whip was the first to sing the beginning: *"Hey, hey..."* The boys all sang together as the music jammed out, *"Bye bye bye (bye, bye bye bye...)"* The music continued and then it went with each guy singing the following parts.

Whip sang the first half of the first verse. Bobi sang the second half. The four boys sang the chorus altogether. Pition sang the first half of the second verse, then he and Bobi both sang the second half. Then all four repeated the chorus and then the rest of the whole song.

They ended the song. The crowd cheered. Gaston grabbed the microphone and spoke again, "There is about enough time for one more song. This ends at about 10:00."

Suddenly, a living skeleton from a science lab brought to life by accident of electricity, showed up. It scared most of the crowd as it walked up to the stage.

"Whoa!" said Gaston in surprise of the skeleton coming up. "Mr. Skeleton, what a surprise! What would like to sing?"

The skeleton grabbed the microphone and said, "I would like to sing 'Taking Care of Business' by BTO."

The disc jockey searched for the correct song. He obviously had every song on the mixed records. He started playing the song. The skeleton followed the music. Then it started singing the first verse and the chorus.

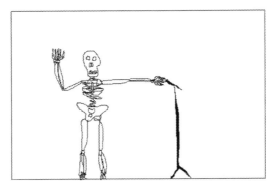

As the music went on, Tehran came by for his son. He barged into the gym and found Whip and his friends. The skeleton continued singing the next verse and repeated the chorus.

"Boys," said Tehran to Whip and his pals, "it's getting late."

"We're about ready," said Whip. He and his friends walked out of the gym as the skeleton kept singing.

The boys followed Tehran outside to the dormitory as Bobi and Pition kept singing some of the songs.

"How was the dance?" asked Tehran.

"Great," said Whip. "We got to sing up on stage and we did an awesome job."

"Glad to hear it," said Tehran.

As they went to the dormitory a meteor lit the night sky as it flew by. The boys went in their dorm and slept for the night.

CHAPTER 20

Another Week Goes By

The next Monday arrived. Whip and his friends studied for upcoming tests. They took them the next few days passing by. The test scores were rather fair. Whip had such a great I.Q. that he would get straight A's. Others would get either a B or a C.

As Tehran tried to build a new career, the Arctics enslaved him into organizing a form in their igloo-like castle. One night, they had a ceremony of a large mead cup for the castle. Angus wore a robe and a helmet with a long spike pointing up, walking down the stairs where the others stood in front of the rails. Tehran was dressed like an old wizard carrying a candle to light the dark basement. Tubbs, dressed in a hooded cloak like a medieval executioner, held the cup. Angus carried a chest of treasure to the table where Tubbs stood by. Tehran carried the candle and set it on the table. Tubbs opened the chest and there were ancient coins and gems. He spread his front limbs with excitement, but accidentally knocked down the candle. It landed on the carpet and fire lit it up.

"Augh! Fire!" Angus screamed. He complained as Tehran grabbed a nearby fire extinguisher and pulled it by the string. He started spraying it all. Soon, the room was dark with no light.

The next morning Whip and his friends were skating by the sidewalk out on the street. They had decided to participate in the Amusers. Suddenly, Angus rode on his skateboard passing by between Whip and Bobi. Fentruck was knocked aside.

"I'll see you at the qualifying rounds, freshmen," said Angus as he continued skating on.

"Hey and after," said Whip, "you'll be bringing me my special kits, dummy!" He and the others continued skating to catch up with Angus.

CHAPTER 21

The College Amusers

The College Amusers was a theme park of rides being installed for new times of opening. They were to be tested by special effort. The workers had stunt people test the waterslides on rubber surfboards with straps for the feet. Sometimes they would have coasters tested with go-karts grinding on rails. Speed wagons were used in racing competitions.

And so, in a locker room in one of the front buildings, Whip and his friends were dressed in water suits and equipped with boots, helmets, pads, and water boards. They were scheduled to test the water sliding ramps in a pool with hills, rails, and steep slopes that curve in a loop. They walked out of the halls to an outside door and exited the building. They walked forward to the image of all the amusers.

"Man," said Whip, "this is everything I dreamed it would be." Some other people were surfing on the waterslides and racing in wagons between walls of mud bricks. Bobi walked after Whip, kneeling to the ground and putting his fists together.

"This place is super-cracking with all the outrage of the nation," he said.

"No kidding," said Pition. "It's larger than what we're used to."

"We'll run this together the right way," said Whip.

"Ohhh!" said a mellow voice bellowing by the heroes. It was Angus with his Arctics joined together in a group, dressed in water suits as well. "I don't think there is anywhere for you to run. We will eat you alive, geniuses."

"Oh, Angus," said Whip. "We're quaking around our boards here."

Suddenly, the speaker came on from a nearby announcement tower: "Attention! One game of Team 10 and Team 47 will be installed with water boarding!"

"That's us," said Whip. "Let's go, guys."

Tehran showed up behind one of the Arctics and waved his arm to his son.

"Good luck, my son," he said.

"Yeah," said Whip, "you too, Dad." He and his friends continued walking to the tower for starting the event as the Arctics followed behind.

The announcer named, Roger, a bulldog, spoke to the audience for the upcoming event, "Hey! Oh, and whaddaya know? Welcome to the water boarding event of the season. We will have our competitors test out the amazing waterslides and fountain hills…" The competitors walked up the stairway to the top of the starting tower. "…and our secondary announcer, Richard Connors will give the report of our competitors."

As Roger spoke, Richard Connors, a gecko, blew in the microphone to test the sound. Then he spoke, "Welcome one and all, today our game will be quite special."

"Plus," Roger interrupted, "one of our newcomers on Team 47 is a mythical creature related to the aardvark, known as the 'psyvark'. He is just about to stand up to Angus Wellington, Jr."

"That's right, Roger!" Richard scolded. "And his name is…"

"Whip…" said Roger, "…Pssssssyyyyy…!" He opened his mouth wide and put his teeth together forming a toothy smile, widening his eyes.

The audience shouted out, "WHIP! WHIP! WHIP!…." They repeated it. Suddenly, Landon Baines showed up in the crowd and said, "Whip, I love you, man!"

As the competitors were gathered in the tower's top floor, Bobi heard the crowd out the side and said, "Nice crowd."

"We've got work to do," said Angus. He gave Tehran a helmet and said, "You do the honors Brother Psy." Then he gave him a water board.

"All right then," said Tehran as he walked forward to the ledge for starting the event.

"Well, well, what do we have here?" said Roger. "The Arctics have a new member who's pretty old for his age."

Tehran looked down at the water pool and sighed, "Oh dear."

"That's right, Roger," said Richard. "Water boarding for the Arctics is…"

"Whip Psy's father, Tehran," said Roger. "He'll have to be equipped before he goes down."

Tehran inserted his feet into the foot straps on the water board. Tubbs came up to lift him when he was ready.

"Whoa ho!" said Whip. "This is gonna be good."

Soon the starting man shot his handgun into the air.

"Ready?" Tubbs asked Tehran as he was about to drop him.

"Yes, go ahead," said Tehran aiming straight for the slide.

"Geronimo!" said Tubbs dropping Tehran. Tehran started riding the board down into the pool. He surfed along the sides and he slid up the fountain in the middle. He was in the air for a few seconds. He splashed into the water below.

Roger announced, "Up the fountain and splash! He's just a bit clumsy." Tehran showed himself underwater upside-down. Then he turned himself up to the surface and got his balance on the board. Roger said, "He's back up and ready to surf some more."

"Looks like Brother Psy needs a boost," said Angus holding a remote on which he pressed a red button to activate rocket boosters strapped on the water board's tail below. The board started to rage across the water pool with waves created behind from the sides as Tehran rode on it fast enough to slide up the steep ramps and through the loops in the pool. Soon he boosted up to where he started.

"He has just made a quick finish," Roger announced, "soon enough to see his current scores."

"That's right, Roger," said Richard. "Those guys on Team 47 are no match for the unbeatable Arctics and their newest member..."

"Tehran Psy!" said Roger. "Let's see what the judges have to say."

The score by the judges were different depending on which country had a unique score. The United States score was 10, so was the United Kingdom, Canada, Italy, France, and Spain. The China score read 11 and the Germany score read 9. The flags were above the display screens.

"We have a lot of 10's!" said Roger. "All except China with 11 and Germany with 9." The crowd cheered for Tehran's score.

"Now it's up to me," said Whip as he walked up to the starting ledge.

"Go for it, lad," said Fentruck.

"We'll count on you," said Bobi.

Whip slid his feet in the straps of his water board. He got ready to move down to the pool.

"It's Whip's turn to surf," said Roger. The starter shot his handgun, and Whip slid down into the water. He moved around the fountain, sliding on walls.

"And here he goes!" said Roger. "He's got quite the moves."

Suddenly, Angus brought out a pocket mirror from inside his water suit. He shone it with the sunlight reflected at the water. As Whip moved within it he blocked his sight because of the brightness. He crashed into a wall and fell backward into the water floating with his board at the surface.

"Sunlight in the water and crash!" said Roger. "That is going to hurt his score." Whip swam back up and got on his board. He continued surfing the pool.

"Here he goes again!" said Roger.

Whip surfed up the walls that curved in a loop and then surfed straight for a bump. He tripped on a lump and slipped on one of the bump's slopes. He bumped his head and fell lying on the dry landing. The crowd gasped.

"Ooh, that has got to hurt," said Roger.

"Come on, Whip!" Pition called to him. "Get up!"

Whip got back up and continued sliding down the slope. He surfed up a wall, and up at the top he did a standing trick with his hands on the edge and his feet in the air. His board was held at the top.

"I've never seen quite a stunt like this," said Roger. "His time is about up." Whip slid down to the pool and surfed back up to the starting ledge.

"And he's done!" said Roger.

Whip sat down and took his board off his feet. He looked at the scoreboard. United States read 7.4; United Kingdom read 7.6; Canada read 4.5; Italy read 5.4; France read 4.3; Spain read 5.6; China read 6.4; and Germany read 5.3.

"What an embarrassment," said Roger. "His scores are between 4 and 8. The Arctics win this event. Better luck next time, Team 47."

Whip carried his board back to the tower's top room as his friends approached him. He felt depressed.

"Cheer up, man," said Bobi.

"Whip, it's okay, dude," said Pition. "We're still in."

Whip huffed and scooted harshly away from them. "Get real!" he scolded.

The crowd shouted out, "Tehran, Tehran, Tehran, Tehran…!" they repeated it.

"Witness, gentlemen," said Angus to his teammates. "Victory's ours. About time we showed those geniuses not to mess with the Arctics."

Some of the crowd people held Tehran over themselves as everyone walked down to the bottom of the tower. The crowd cheered and cheered for Tehran as they repeated his name. Whip was walking away as his father witnessed him.

"Whip! Where are you going!" he called. Whip seemed guilty of losing the event. He and his friends left the park through the crowd.

CHAPTER 22

Mobi and Maudi's Suspension

Before I can tell the story about Whip and his father separating again, I have to tell you *this* story in East Boundary Elementary School. It was recess and Bobi's young twin brothers, Mobi and Maudi, were up to no good. They held a camera. Jessica Pawston, a bear cub, was about to use the bathroom and she walked in. Mobi and Maudi snuck behind bushes on their secret mission into the girls' bathroom. Campus supervisors walked through the hall and onto the playground. Mobi and Maudi walked to a nearby drinking fountain, making sure there was nobody else around.

"The coast is clear," said Mobi. They snuck into the girls' bathroom, slowly sneaking up by the stall where Jessica used a toilet. Maudi activated the camera ready for a snapshot. Mobi used a coin from his pocket to unlock the door. He quickly opened it as Maudi took a picture of Jessica on the toilet. They both started laughing as Jessica screamed out.

"HEY!" she shouted. "YOU BOYS ARE IN HUGE TROUBLE! YOU KNOW YOU'RE IN THE WRONG BATHROOM!"

Mobi and Maudi continued laughing as Mobi took the camera to take another picture. They dashed out the door.

"You boys are gonna get expelled or something!" Jessica called to them. Mobi and Maudi continued their long giggle as they darted behind a bush in a nearby planter.

And so, a moment passed as Jessica finished using the restroom. She walked to the front office to talk to the principal about the situation.

"Were in big trouble," said Maudi as he noticed the next event after their scheme. Mobi and Maudi went out onto the playground. They shot some basketball hoops. Soon it was time to line up. Mobi and Maudi were led into their first grade class. As they were in the phone rang. Their new teacher, Ms. Longyear, answered it. It was the principal calling. As the call was finished, Ms. Longyear hung it up and went towards Mobi and Maudi and said, "The principal wants to see you."

Mobi and Maudi were dismissed. They walked to the front office to meet the principal, Miss Humberg.

"I heard that you boys have gotten in serious trouble today," she said.

"Um," said Mobi. "Yeah, we were playing a joke by taking pictures in the girls' bathroom."

"Well, you're in the blowout of the school's law," said the principal.

The assistant principal, Mr. Pallin, came into the office and said, "You boys are going to be suspended for three days. And you must promise to never go in the girls' bathroom again for any purpose. Is that clear?"

"Yes, sir," said Mobi and Maudi.

"Let me call your mom," said Mr. Pallin. He grabbed the phone and called the Gatorsons' house. Mrs. Harley Gatorson had just driven home after teaching choir at the same school. The phone rang and she answered it. When she heard the principal's message about the boys' trouble-making scheme, she became angry and drove back to pick up her twin sons.

CHAPTER 23

A Hard Time For a Father and Son

Meanwhile back in college, at the University, Whip walked to different places just to stay away from his father because of the event. Tehran showed up and found his son.

"Whip, there you are!" he said. "I've been looking everywhere for you. Where have you been?"

"Just save your energy," said Whip. "You may have won the event last weekend, but Dad…" He huffed and puffed. "…this campus is just not big enough for both of us."

"I'm not concerned about the campus," said Tehran. "I'm only trying to see where you're going and what you're up to."

"I'm just trying to look for a job, Dad," said Whip. "I just feel uncomfortable with you around me. Those Arctics are trying to make you win around me."

"I didn't mean to turn it out that way, Whip. I was just trying to be a bit like you."

Whip made an angry growl and said, "Don't you get it? I'm trying to be unique around here! And I don't need any of your help! I'm not a little kid anymore, so just stay away from me and *get your own life!*" He walked away.

"Fine!" said Tehran.

Hours later there was a test that day in the American Government classroom. The professor, James Lincoln, announced, "Alright students your test is studied well. It is time to start." Tehran came at the door and entered. "You may open," said the professor.

Tehran walked down the classroom for his seat.

"Well, Mr. Psy," said the professor. "We are about to have a test so you'll have to study for it while I pass it out."

Tehran sat down and quickly looked at his studied notes for the test. He used a magic force to zoom and scan all the information. The professor passed envelopes to all the students in the classroom. Soon everything was set. Everyone was ready. Tehran put his notes away when he was done.

"You may open your envelopes and begin," said Professor Lincoln.

The people in the class took out their examinations. They wrote their names and what college they were in. And so, they all started taking the test. As it all happened, Tehran looked around himself and found his son sitting far back with his friends. The professor came by Tehran and said, "No wandering eyes, sir."

As Tehran answered questions on the test, thoughts arose in his head. He daydreamed of his son floating like a cloud saving other mythical creatures like a hero. A song occurred that nobody has heard of:

"My world is in peril and I must refuge
There is nobody like me and I am not to lose
I lost myself in battle I will no longer suffer
The war is won and fought for and I can't see my succor

So, I'm a myth, I'm a myth, yes, I am a myth
I will spread my mercy as one of my special gifts."

In the daydream, Tehran sat at a picnic table having a cup of tea in a saucer. Whip appeared at the other end of the table from his father. He grabbed the pitcher in the middle of the table to pour himself a cup of tea.

"Dad," he said as he took a drink, "you never seem too far away, but you're still here with me."

"As I assure you, my son," said Tehran.

Suddenly, Whip transformed into a different figure. He then appeared as the long-eared, small-snouted, mustached creature called a Vip. His body turned out fat. Tehran gasped at the sight.

"Brendor?" he whimpered.

"You're finished, Tehran Psy!" growled the Vip. He harshly grabbed the table cloth and swept the dishes off it. Tehran fell backwards into a bottomless down way. Memories came by as he fell into an illusion.

"Yoooooouuuuu'rrrrre FFFIIIIIIIIIIRRRRRRRRRED!" shouted the memory of the rhinoceros boss from the office where Tehran was fired from. Next memory was the van beeping with the boys driving to college from home. Tehran mumbled about the memories.

"I have noticed you don't have a college degree," said the memory with Mrs. Prunella Woods.

"Just think," said the memory with Pittz Vipers. "I'll be a free snake when I'm through with my job! Oh yeah!"

Suddenly, Tehran landed on an appearing trampoline that bounced him up and he landed on a faraway ground that seemed solid white and his head was out of control. He fell asleep for a minute, and then he woke up and sighed.

"Get your own life!" shouted a voice from the sky. Tehran shook his head when he heard it. It was his son. Tehran looked around as his son's voice shouted, "Get your own life!" Tehran found him up at the ceiling.

"Leave me alone and get your own life!" Whip said as he slammed the ceiling's door. Tehran put his hand to his forehead and continued his test. He had already finished most of the exercises he was getting to the end.

"Pencils down!" a voice called out behind Tehran's mind. It was Professor Lincoln. Tehran found his face.

"I said," said the professor, "pencils down."

Tehran stopped daydreaming. He put his pencil down and the professor grabbed his test.

"Well, I'm not finished," said Tehran. "I only have ten exercises left."

"I'm sorry, Mr. Psy," said the professor. "But it's over already." He walked with the papers to his desk as the students walked out the backdoor. Tehran left his desk and exited the room.

Moments later, Tehran sat on the bench by the fountain outside in the university's campus field. People walked around and many waved their hands to Tehran. He waved back. He sat there for an hour or two. Memories flowed through his head with the past of him and his son together. He later got ready to leave the university. He decided to drive home to sleep in his room later that night.

CHAPTER 24

Lab Brats

And so, back in Eastern Boundary Elementary School, the third graders were in another classroom about to dissect a cow's eye, create a hand-made telescope, and so on. Sarah Psy always thought that animal dissections were totally disgusting. So she went to participate in the instructions of making small telescopes out of paper towel rolls.

"This seems easy," she said. She listened to the teacher's instructions by grabbing a roll, poking a hole in a piece of wax paper, and taping it on one end. Finally, she had to put a holed piece of aluminum foil on the other end.

"Which end do I look through?" Sarah asked the teacher.

"The wax paper end," said the teacher. Sarah looked through the telescope.

"It turns the image upside-down," said Sarah.

"Exactly," said the teacher.

"This is ridiculous. This kind of science makes me feel stupid."

"Don't go too hard on it, honey. There is a lot of science that historical people discovered that goes in a different path."

Meanwhile, a raccoon boy named, Quasimodo Fletcher, participated in the eye dissection.

"This is cool," he said. "I never could figure out what was inside an animal's eyeball before." As he looked at the cow's eye on the newspaper lying on the table, he grabbed a razor blade next to him and started cutting the eye open. The juice from inside spilled.

"Ah man!" said Quasimodo. "This is totally cool! I never imagined such gross stuff so smelly and slimy."

Suddenly, Jessica Pawston looked at Quasimodo's experiment and said, "You're disgusting, Quasi!"

"So," said Quasimodo, "what difference does it make?" He put one digit, wearing gloves, into the eye juice and flicked it at Jessica.

"Ewww!" she shouted as a little drop barely touched her. "*That* kind of difference."

"Kids!" a nearby teacher cried out. "What's all this quarrel about?"

"Quasimodo's being a geek," said Jessica. "He just flicked some eye juice on me!"

"Did not!" Quasimodo shouted. "I was just trying to work."

"Kids!" the teacher said aloud. "Let's not mess around like that, just mind your own business." The young animals went back to their work.

Random Announcer speaking: "You know, some kids don't always get used to the idea of something gross that lives inside them. So those of you, readers, who have no fear in biology should always get used to the idea."

CHAPTER 25

Tehran's Guilt

Now, the next day, Tehran decided to think of himself and his son as he sat on a bench in the park behind all the neighbors' houses as Pittz was cooking hamburgers and hot dogs for the kids playing on the castle in the bark pit.

"Oh, Pittz," Tehran whimpered, "what am I gonna do now?"

"Ah, relax, Tehran, it's no big deal," said Pittz. "It usually takes time to think about things, especially for me if *I* want to get my family together."

"Well, *that* makes sense," said Tehran. "My son's been ditching me the past two days."

Pittz stopped cooking the food and set the finished patties and hot dogs on a nearby platter. Then he grabbed some darts and an outdoor target stand. He slid out of his robot suit and grabbed the darts with his tail from his robot's hand.

"If you know that three strikes take one person out," he explained to Tehran, "you'll survive." He threw one dart, which hit the target's inner ring. "Anyone can win in any direction." He threw another dart and laughed. "Take it from me, sir!"

Tehran's mind grew strong. A thought rose in his head saying, "If you want to make a degree, you must stay focused on your goal for life." He quickly grabbed the last dart from Pittz's tail and focused it on the target. He aimed for the center and threw the dart. He used magic in his eyes to make a bull's eye. The dart hit the center.

"Yes!" Tehran shouted. "My goal is complete." He grabbed Pittz's head in excitement. "I've got my focus back. Now I must return for my son." He dropped Pittz and ran to his car. He drove away to the University. Pittz had something on his mind as Tehran drove away.

"Did I miss something?" he asked himself.

CHAPTER 26

A New Plan for the Whip Team

And so, back by the University at the "A Petít Fraîche" bar, Whip was walking there on the sidewalk as it started raining. A human girl walked by and said, "Hey, I've seen you before. Aren't you…?"

"Yeah," said Whip. "Whip Psy."

"I saw your father water skating," said the girl moving her arms in excitement. "He is so radical like you!"

"Yeah," said Whip, "sort of."

Rain poured down. The girl spread out her umbrella as Whip put his hood over his head. His friends waited for him in the bar. Inside, Bobi explained something unnatural and unexpected.

"The Arctics have some practical devices that make them cheat," he said. "There must be a way for us geniuses to outsmart them."

"Bleeding Kansas," said Fentruck, "that makes the perfect sense we need."

"You don't hear about that stuff every day," said Pition. Whip walked down the entrance stairs.

"Hey, guys," he said to his friends.

"Whip," said Pition as he slithered toward him. "We have an ingenious plan. We can outsmart those Arctics by making them give up. They have cheated for years with devices. That's what Bobi said."

"Thanks for the advice, Pit," said Whip. "I lost in my best event."

"Don't take it so hard, Whip," said Bobi approaching him. "Where have you been, buddy? We can't give up, you know."

"Look, guys," said Whip. "It's for the victory. Those Arctics are going nowhere but to trouble." He tried walking outside of the bar. The French girl who sang for the bar was drinking coffee. Thoughts about Whip came in her head.

"Whip, Whip, Whip," she said. "Admit defeat…" Whip listened to her and slowly walked toward her. "…and defeat will surely conquer your specimen. If the Arctics can't win then you must."

"Alright," said Whip as he settled himself on a nearby table. He grabbed a cup of coffee. "I couldn't even beat my father, who was thought to be the most mysteriously athletic challenge man in mythology. How can you expect me to beat the other competitors?! We're starting in last place because of *me!*"

Bobi approached him and said, "That never stopped you before, Whip…or the rest of us. Do you want that Arctic fox geek, Angus Wellington, Jr., to satisfy your habits?"

Whip answered, "No."

"Are you ever gonna let us down for if someone else is your old man?" Bobi asked.

"No!" Whip said.

"Are you gonna be someone else's bus booooooyyyyyy?!"

"No I'm not! I'm not cleaning up anybody's stupid mess."

"That's what I like to hear."

"Together we can do it," said Pition.

"You're right," said Whip. "We can still beat 'em!"

"Hands and tail up," said Fentruck as he put his front flipper in the center within the group. Pition put his tail on it as Bobi and Whip put their hands there, too.

"Yeah!" said Bobi out loud. "Talk about a mission possible!"

The guys lifted their appendages, shouting, "Let's do it…" then they smacked them all above themselves. "…TO IT!" They all ran out of the bar in excitement. They headed back to the university. The French girl continued drinking her coffee.

"Boys are boys while girls are girls," she said.

CHAPTER 27

Getting the Grades Up

And so, the plan was coming together. The boys were in the library studying for next tests and doing other homework. Landon came by.

"Hey, guys," he said.

"Landon," said Bobi. "You were sexy while singing that karaoke song on stage."

"Thanks, dude," said Landon.

"We'll see you around," said Whip. "We've got work to do."

"So do I," said Landon as he walked away to do his homework getting a reference book.

Meanwhile, Tehran was outside praying that his son would agree to be with him with no problems anymore. He was on his knees kneeling in front of a clay bench with his hands held together.

"Lord Almighty, my creator," he said, "make my son not angry but happy when I'm with him. I only want to help him get through this year. Please let him know this. Amen." He stopped praying and headed back inside the library. "I must get my grades up," he said to himself, "and quit those stupid Arctics and most importantly I get my son back!" He entered the library and decided to get some work done.

The next day, Tehran had some homework done and then he needed exercise in a rec room. He started running on a running machine activating its conveyor at 10 miles an hour. He could never stop his speed of mythology.

Later, Whip, Bobi, Pition, and Fentruck entered the exercise room and Tehran finished using the running machine. Whip got onto it. Bobi set himself on a nearby flat bed and started lifting a heavy weight up and down. Pition slithered up and hooked his upper jaw on a pull-up bar and lifted his body up and down. Fentruck used a hula hoop with massaging points around his belly spinning it around. The song "Let's Get It Started" by the Black-Eyed Peas played on the radio nearby.

After a lot of exercise, they all studied homework for an upcoming test. All this work with raising grades went on for weeks.

October arrived. The boys went to check their grades in the hallway on a bulletin board. There were mostly A's.

"I have all A's," said Whip.

"Way to go, Whip," said Bobi, "I have three A's and two B's."

"I have four A's and one B," said Pition.

"I have two A's, two B's, and one C," said Fentruck.

"Hey," said Whip, "my dad has all A's, too."

"What a family of wise creatures like you," said Pition. Suddenly, Tehran walked by to see his grades.

"Dad, we're on the same track," said Whip. "We both have all A's."

"Hail the conquering heroes," said Fentruck.

"What are we gonna do, now?" asked Bobi.

"Well," said Tehran. "I still have a few more things to take care of."

"Let's go, guys," said Whip as he and his friends left the hallway. Tehran stood there alone to think about what should be done and what mistakes he could take back.

CHAPTER 28

Tehran Quits the Arctics

Figuring out everything he had done, Tehran went back to the Arctic igloo as Angus played pool with one of his teammates, the elephant seal.

"So, Brother Tehran," said Angus, "hopefully you've been working hard in the university lately."

"Yes," said Tehran, "but you see, the thing is…that I have to get off this team."

"I see," said Angus as he took a shot. Suddenly he had a distraction. He had the idea come to this head and tossed his stick across the table. Then he said, "Excuse me," turning to Tehran.

"You *what?*" asked the elephant seal.

"I know what you're thinking, dude," said the big horn sheep on the couch nearby reading a magazine.

"What is he talking about, huh?" asked the snowy owl flapping his wings over the pool table.

"You say you want to leave us behind and go off on your own?" Angus asked Tehran.

"Not exactly," said Tehran, "I've got better plans than being with you."

"So you want to ditch us on the last day of the competition, eh?" Angus asked.

Tehran backed up and bumped into Tubbs's belly. Tubbs lifted him up with his paw holding his head.

"We can knock the sense out of his big brain of legend," Tubbs said.

"Whoa, whoa, whoa, hey down, Tubbs," said Angus as he grabbed a pool stick behind him and waved his hand, "easy there, big boy." He poked the stick into one of Tehran's nostrils. "Now, Tehran, if you think you're quitting the Arctics to join that freshman genius son of yours,…" he pulled the stick out. "…you've got another thing coming to you." He poked the stick into Tehran's belly.

"Bull's eye, man!" said Tubbs giggling. "That bad boy's in trouble and his daddy's gonna lock him up in the cellar!" He laughed and so did the other Arctics.

Tehran frowned and said, "Not a chance, you muggers!" He quickly grabbed the stick from Angus's paws and used it to poke the fat end fast onto Tubbs's toes.

"DAUGH!" Tubbs screamed in pain. "Ow, my paw! Ow, my paw!" He dropped Tehran to the floor and ran off. All the other Arctics were shocked by the whole fighting scene. Tehran and Angus wrestled each other with the stick in their clutching appendages.

"I'm not going to be on anyone's team!" said Tehran.

Angus jumped on the table with a side-step as he looked at Tehran. "You're such a wise old man, Teh," he said. "But you forgot one thing…" he whispered, "Nobody. I repeat…" He spoke out loud, "Nobody quits the Arctics!" He made a toothy frown. Tehran threw the stick out of the way as Angus leaped off the table.

"If you don't know that I have rights of whatever I want to do," Tehran scolded, "you should be ashamed of yourself. You should see a judge in court. I'm leaving the Arctics and that's everything." He tried to exit the igloo, but two Arctics made a stopping X with pool sticks to stop him.

"Actually, you are *not* leaving the Arctics, Tehran Psy," said Angus.

All of the Arctics grabbed Tehran from his feet to his head and carried him out the exit door. They altogether threw him out into the street. Tehran screamed and landed on the asphalt road by the other side from the igloo.

"You're lucky I'm just a myth!" he called back to the Arctics. "I don't break!"

"The Arctics are leaving you out here!" Angus called to him.

"Sayonara!" said the big horn sheep.

"Hasta la vista, mister!" said the snowy owl. The Arctics closed the igloo's door.

Tehran stood back up. "They're through with me already," he said. He suddenly felt something on his chest pocket. "Ah," he said. "Forgot to return my Arctic pin." He walked back to the igloo. He entered the front foyer and set his pin on a nearby side table with a mirror. He looked in it and saw the Arctics back in the billiard room. They had an evil discussion.

"So, gentlemen," said Angus. "You all know what we've always done to flush those freshmen out of our way in winning every competition."

"Yeah," said the big horn sheep. "We always cheat."

"Cheat," said the others. "Cheat. Cheat. Cheat."

"Just like we did last time, guys," said Tubbs.

Angus moved in front of the fireplace. "And that was a great cheat," he said. He turned to his teammates and said, "Now, I have a better plan." He made a wide, evil grin with a red glow of fire behind him.

"I've got to warn my son and the others," said Tehran in the hallway. He snuck out of the igloo and ran back to the university.

CHAPTER 29

Championship Time

Inside the university's locker room, Whip and his pals grabbed their equipment and clothing for the final competition of the College Amusers.

"This is it, guys," said Whip. "Championship time." He tied the lace on one of the large, thick, waterproof sporting shoes.

"It's time to kick some bad guy booty," said Bobi, putting on *his* shoes.

"It's a good thing people know about citizen snakes," said Pition as he grabbed a flexible tunnel-like suit out of his locker. He slid inside from the tail end to the head end to put it on. "Perfect fit," he said.

"Helmet, check," said Whip. "T-shirt, check. Elbow pads, check. Fingerless gloves, check. Shorts, check. Knee pads, check. Thick sport shoes, check. Everybody have everything?"

"Yeah," said Bobi, Pition, and Fentruck, altogether. Suddenly, Tehran came by and opened the door.

"Huh? Oh," said Pition. "Hi, Mr. Psy."

"What's up, Tehran?" asked Fentruck.

Tehran entered the room and walked toward Whip saying, "Whip, I came to warn you that the Arctics have been cheating all along."

"That's what *I've* been saying," said Bobi.

"Some genius you are, Bobe," said Pition.

"Did Angus tell you to say that?" Whip asked his father. "Dad, I don't have time for this, I need to stay focused." He walked out of the locker room with his friends.

"Well, good luck," said Tehran. "You'll figure everything out."

83

CHAPTER 30

The Big Competitions

And so, everybody was ready for the championship league. They went back to the College Amusers to participate in the upcoming events. Roger the announcer spoke out, "Oh, ladies and gentlemen! Welcome back to the College Amusers." There were players doing tricks on the water ramps and roller coaster rails. "The excitement is about to come forth," Roger announced as a player crashed through a wooden wall while riding a bumper car. "Sit back and relax. It's the College Amusers!" Roger was speaking from inside of a blimp's carriage. A giant video screen was on the side. "From here and BEYOND!" Roger spoke out loud. "Already now, let's have a roundabout with the events for the Amusers' championship."

"That's right, Roger," said Richard Connors announcing by the Amusers' ground. "Our game of the main event will begin any moment. We'll see bungee-jumping, hovercrafts, and much more." Roger turned off the communication connected inside the blimp.

"Won't that be fun?" he said. A sign of the Arctics showed up. "First off we announce Team 10: the Arctics; four of them today, Angus Wellington, Jr., Tubbs the polar bear, Sir Puffer the puffin, and Wahoo Yahoo." Wahoo Yahoo was a fish called a wahoo, with the Arctics. He was held in a tank with robot limbs for sporting. Suddenly, the audience moaned with a problem.

"What happened to Tehran!" they shouted.

"Well, it looks like Tehran Psy is a no-show," said Richard Connors.

Suddenly, a guy with no shirt, wearing a turban ran around passing Richard and shouted, "WHAT HAPPENED TO TEH-MAN!"

Meanwhile, Whip and his pals along with the Arctics stood in a waiting post. Whip spoke to Angus, "Hey, Angus! What did you do with my dad?!"

"He decided to quit," said Angus. "You see? He was never a piece of Arctic material."

Tehran was alone and helpless. He wandered around the Amusers' crowd aisles and inside several locker rooms. He felt depressed.

Back at the Amusers' field, Roger announced, "Now for the semifinal round, we will start with bungee-jumping."

Bobi participated in the event. He tied a bungee cord around his ankles and so did two other competitors. They all jumped down from a height over a pool of water.

"Whhhooooooaaaa, Nelly!" Bobi shouted as he fell toward the pool. He suddenly bounced back up along with the others. A white ferret from the Arctics' team brought a boomerang that he threw toward the competitors. One of them dodged it until it cut another player's cord. That player screamed and fell all the way down to the pool. The boomerang went back to the ferret. Whip, Pition, and Fentruck saw the player fall in the safety pool. The ferret laughed. Bobi was falling again. The ferret threw the boomerang again. As it passed Bobi moved back to avoid it. He had an idea. He grabbed his cord and climbed up avoiding the boomerang. He climbed up a few yards then he fell letting go of the cord. He bounced up high and back up to the starting platform. The ferret threw the boomerang again. Bobi reached for the platform scooting forward, flapping his arms. The boomerang cut his cord. Bobi grabbed the platform's edge. He climbed up and then stood up and shouted, "YEAH! WHO'S YOUR GATOR?!" He whistled with digits in his mouth. The audience cheered.

The next event was a hovercraft race. Whip buckled into a yellow hovercraft in front of him. Another player beside him buckled into a green hovercraft. The gun was blown and the two racers ran their crafts into the water path that went in a squiggled line and certain zigzags. Suddenly, the Arctics brought a bag of piranhas which they opened in the water. The piranhas raged out on the loose.

"Huh?" Whip said in surprise. The racer in the green craft hopped over the piranhas one by one. Whip tried zooming across the water with speed. A piranha bit a hole in the green hovercraft's tube. It spewed much air that the racer tried moving to safety as Whip passed through the zigzag on top of the hay bale walls then back in the water. The other racer jumped to a hay bale and climbed out of the race to escape the piranhas. Whip reached the finish line with a muddy shore. The audience cheered again.

The next event was jumping with pogo sticks. Pition was coiled around one while three other players joined the event. The gun was shot. Pition and the others bounced up a hill with platforms sticking out. The Arctics brought boxes of firecrackers. They waited for the players to jump on high platforms. Then they threw the firecrackers they lit to distract the players.

"Yikes!" shouted a player as a firecracker exploded. Just then Pition quickly bounced and bounced from platform to platform as more firecrackers were thrown. He dodged them all and reached the top of the hill. He slid off the pogo stick and waved his head and tail in the air. The crowd cheered again.

The final event was parachuting. Fentruck was to participate in it (although he is a heavy-weighted walrus). He and others had to ride a long way up on an elevator from the ground up to the top of a tall tower.

"Man, that's a sure long way up," said Bobi back on Earth. Suddenly, the Arctics brought fireworks to distract the parachuters. The participants were about to reach the top. The big horn sheep set out some fireworks on rods. The snowy owl grabbed some matches and tried lighting the fireworks as the parachuters were at the top. The big horn sheep quickly blew out the matches.

"Wait 'til they jump out, you retard," he said.

"Sorry," said the owl.

The parachuters jumped and their parachutes spread out. Fentruck tried not to fear the long way down to the target below. He seemed heavy to a parachute. The Arctics lit the fireworks and launched them up at the air with the parachuters. They exploded and sparks burned holes in their parachutes.

"Bleeding Kansas!" said Fentruck as he looked up at the others ascending with fire then descending. Fentruck was the fastest descender with the most weight. Seconds later he and the others landed on the target at the same time. Fentruck was proclaimed the best survivor of the disaster of fireworks. The crowd cheered.

"And so," Roger announced, "we have our winners for Team 47 and some other players were damaged by hostile devices." The hurt players were taken to a medical tent. Angus, standing nearby, took off his helmet and grinned and winked at his fellow Arctics. He put one thumb up.

"Yeah," said the Arctics.

CHAPTER 31

The Bad Start

"And now, ladies and gentlemen," Roger announced, "it's time for our final event called the College Amusers' triathlon. First we start with the jet ski race."

The players were placed on the high, flat top deck of a ramp where jet skis were placed. They were in a pool at the top and the players were about to walk onto them to leap down to the water below. The referee, a human with a goatee, looked at his watch to keep track of the time until it was time to start.

"Take your positions," the referee said as the players climbed on their jet skis. "On your mark..." Suddenly, Angus had a remote control that made rockets start firing. The referee continued, "...get set..." Angus pressed the remote's button. Fentruck's jet ski started blasting ahead of everyone else. Then he was lost out in the water. The referee blew his whistle. "Bad start! Bad start! Team 47, get over here."

"Wait! Hold on," said Whip as he dismounted his jet ski. "Angus just blasted our fourth player ahead of us."

"Well, that was ludicrous," said Angus, "I didn't do anything; I was just standing here for no reason."

"Oh great," Whip sighed. "Now we have an opening on our team."

"I told you those Arctics had devices," said Bobi.

"Bobi's right," said Whip as he pointed to the Arctics, "you guys are cheating! That's what my dad's been trying to tell me."

"Can we get on with the race, please?" asked Angus. "Wait a minute, uh…" he counted Whip's team. "…one, two, three, oh you don't seem to have enough team members now, do you."

"Rules are rules," said the referee. "You have to be a full team or you'll have to forfeit to your opponents."

"Wait! That's not fair!" Whip exclaimed. "We don't know anybody around there." Suddenly, the blimp moved over the starting ramp. Richard Connors spoke on the screen, "Oh! It seems we have a little trio here, folks." Whip found him on a nearby platform at the corner of the deck. Richard Connors continued, "Team 47, short at hand, will be disqualified in just about two minutes." Whip knocked him away and grabbed the microphone, speaking in front of the camera, "Dad, it's me, Whip. If you're out there somewhere…"

Tehran found his son from the crowd speaking on the blimp's screen.

"Oh no," he said, "my son's up to no good." The crowd merely gasped.

"Dad, relax," said Whip, "Everything's normal, it's just that my team needs you…" he sighed. "…in fact, *I* need you."

"What do you know?" Tehran asked a crowd member. "I've got to help my son." He felt his left hip pocket with a dart. "I've got my lucky dart for a case of an emergency." He dashed down the stairs. "I'M COMING, WHIP!" He reached a rail on the front of the audience's seat aisle. He leaped over it and used his magic to shift himself into a comet. He shot away like a meteor. The audience seemed shocked at the sight.

Back at the starting ramp, Whip settled himself on a rail at the back.

"You know, Whip," said Bobi, "I don't think your dad's gonna make it."

"Well, if he doesn't," said Whip, "then we're definitely screwed up."

"Okay," said Angus to the referee. "I guess these guys are finished."

"No, not yet," said the referee. "They still have a minute."

Whip and his pals waited a few seconds for Tehran to show. Suddenly, Pition saw a shining comet nearby.

"Hey, what's that?" he asked. "It looks like a comet with a zigzagging body."

"That must be one of my species' magic tricks," said Whip, "the Psy-Comet. It's probably my dad coming." The comet moved closer.

"METEOR SHOWER!" shouted the Arctics as the jumped off their jet skis. The comet landed smoothly and disappeared. It was Tehran who made it in time.

"Ta daaaaaaa!" he said.

"Dad!" Whip said as he walked to him. The audience cheered aloud. Angus went by the referee grabbing his shoulders and complained, "Oh, please don't accept him, he's finished!"

"Not by my rules," said the referee backing up Angus.

"Whip," Tehran said to his son, "I have much to tell you."

"Dad," said Whip. "Why don't we get on with this race first?"

"As you wish," said Tehran. The players went back on their jet skis and waited for the time to start. Tehran got his own jet ski extra from a shop.

CHAPTER 32

The Triathlon Goes On

"**T**ake your positions," said the referee looking at his watch. "On your marks, get set…" He blew his pistol. The racers zoomed down to the water below and started racing.

"This is way more fun than swimming with my own kind," said Wahoo Yahoo.

"I must say," said Pition with his mouth on the jet ski's handle, "dis is ridiculous. I can't moob my body side to side." He had to keep his tail on the acceleration pedal. The Arctics started speeding ahead along with Whip.

"This is my race, Angus!" Whip called to him.

"Not for long," said Angus as he started turning to the path ahead then so did the rest of the racers. He grabbed a walkie-talkie he had in his shorts' hip pocket. He pressed the button and spoke, "Operation floatie… up ahead." The white ferret held the other walkie-talkie.

"Aye-aye, Captain," he said. He activated a pump to put air in a floatie nearby. When it was full, he set it in the water and sat on it. He wore a pair of sun shades. The floatie moved around on the surface.

"Uh oh, we have a floater on the road," Roger spoke. "We better be aware audiences not to go in front of our competitors." The Arctics passed the ferret.

"Whoa!" said Whip. "Pass him, guys!" He and his friends went around the ferret, but Tehran ran into him. The ferret climbed up to Tehran.

"Oh," Tehran said as he noticed him. "Sorry about that." The ferret bit his arm nearby. "OW!" Tehran shouted. "Get off me!" He waved his arm around and threw the ferret into a nearby forest of trees. The ferret landed on a branch and ran into the upper body segment.

"Ow!" he said. "Landed in a stupid tree."

Back in the race the others were making their way through different directions.

"You'll never catch me this time, Whip!" Angus called to him from one side of an isle in the race.

"We'll see about that!" Whip called back from the other side. They kept racing ahead of every isle in the path. Just then, Angus changed his walkie-talkie to another channel and pressed the button and spoke, "Operation waterfall." It was connected to the other walkie-talkie with the other Arctics by the side rail. The elephant seal spoke out to the crowd, "Ain't that an albatross up there?!"

The crowd said, "Albatross? Where?!" They turned their heads to the sky as the big horn sheep pressed a button that lifted buoys up from the side to show the heroes their doom. It caught their attention. They went down there.

"Team 47 has just hit the detour," said Roger. Whip and his friends followed the way down the falls to a lower road in the race. Tehran shot himself ahead and passed his son. The Arctics raced through a tunnel on the previous part of the race. Whip, Bobi, and Pition landed just ahead of them. They went into a loop ahead.

"Hey, no fair!" exclaimed Tubbs. "They cheated!" The Arctics continued their path. They hurried to catch up with the heroes by jumping down with their jet skis to the next level. Suddenly, Tehran landed on Sir Puffer's jet ski and crashed.

"Excuse me," said Tehran as he got up and sped away. Sir Puffer swam up and began flying.

"Luckily, I'm a bird that can fly!" he shouted. So he flew out of the race as the others continued on.

Angus ran beside Tubbs and said, "Throw me ahead, Tubbs!" Tubbs grabbed Angus's handlebar and spun around. Then he launched Angus ahead of the heroes.

"So long, suckers!" Tubbs shouted as he spread his arms pushing Whip and Bobi down forward. They turned upside-down in the water but got back up. Pition continued ahead. Whip and Bobi caught up as fast as they could as Tehran did also.

Soon, the first part of the triathlon was nearly over the next part is using gliders. As the racers reached a muddy shore, the big horn sheep, hiding under a bush, adjusted one of the bolts on one of the gliders. The racers dismounted their jet skis. The big horn sheep went to a hiding place and kept the bush still. The racers came to the gliders.

"Off of the jet skis and onto the gliders," Roger announced. Angus, Whip, and Bobi were the first three to glide. Pition, Tubbs, and Wahoo Yahoo were next. Tehran was the last one.

"Whoa!" he shouted as he looked at the ground below.

"Sorry, Dad!" Whip called to him. "I forgot that you hate flying!"

"I don't mind flying!" Tehran said. "I just hate heights!"

"Cool tuna!" said Bobi. "Look at that ground below! It's like flying paradise, man!" Suddenly, the bolt on his glider was about to loosen. Sir Puffer flew by his teammates.

"You need a bit of effort!" he said to Angus. He flew on Angus's glider and used some strength to lift up the wings.

As Whip and his teammates kept gliding and having to turn at some points to the next platform, Bobi's glider started to come apart when the bolt shot out. He held onto the bars until when they were reaching the next platform, Bobi fell down into a puddle of mud below.

"Whoa! Augh!" he screamed.

"Ooh, look out!" said Roger. "Bobert Gatorson is down and 'SPLASH!' into the mud." The other players reached the landing platform and went off their gliders. Whip turned down to Bobi.

"Bobi!" he called down to him. "Are you all right?!"

"Keep going, Whip!" Bobi called back. "I'm just in a bunch of mud!"

Whip scurried to the Arctics with an illusive run as his father was the last to land on the platform and take off his glider. Whip was scooting ahead with his illusion trick to get ahead of the Arctics. The Arctics ran after him as Pition made a fast slither and Tehran ran afterwards.

The final part was about to come. The racers were climbing up a wall of ladder bars. It seemed pretty high. At the top were non-coaster wagons which are used to race down a road with no rails.

"And now," Roger announced, "the final part of the triathlon is the anti-coaster wagon race. Using front handles for steering."

The racers got up to the top of the wall. They got into the wagons that stood in front of them near the edge. Whip, Pition, and the Arctics entered the wagons and started rolling down a high ramp. They followed a squiggled path down its trail. Tehran rolled his chosen wagon toward the edge, remembering that he hated heights. All of a sudden he started rolling down to follow the others. He screamed and panicked. Then suddenly, he ran into a wall and flipped out of the wagon. The other racers reached the end of the squiggled road. Tehran crash-landed on Angus, knocking him out of his wagon.

"Wow!" said Roger. "It looks like Angus and Tehran caused a collision course."

Angus tumbled on the road ahead as Tehran landed with his belly on a nearby hay bale liner. The rest of the racers kept moving. Angus woke up.

"Huh?" he said as he saw the others ahead. "Tubbs! Wait for me!" Tubbs did not hear him. Angus grew angry. "I can't be ignored. I'm king of this course." He stood up with a remote for rockets. He pointed toward the racers ahead. "Nobody finishes this race but ME!"

"Oh no!" shouted Tehran as he saw Angus with the remote. "Whip!" He took out his lucky dart from his hip pocket and said, "You must keep eye on target without cheating!" He threw it at Angus's face. Angus turned to it. Its needle poked in his muzzle.

"OOOOOWWWWW!" he screamed in pain. "Son of a—" He tried pulling it out. As he did, he slammed his paw on the remote's button. It activated the rocket on Whip's wagon. He blasted ahead toward Tubbs.

"Whoa!" he said.

"What the—" said Tubbs. Whip collided with his wagon. They headed for the bottom right leg of the giant letter A in the middle of the road. They screamed together and crashed. The rocket's engine lit the A on fire. The letter fell down. The audience was unsatisfied at the sight.

"Another collision!" said Roger.

"NOOOOOOO!" Tehran shouted. "Here I come, Whip!" He ran toward the wreck.

"Wait for me!" Pition called to him slithering fast.

Angus threw the dart out of the race. Then he grinned and thought of an evil idea about the wreck. Wahoo Yahoo's tank was broken he flipped around as he was out of water.

"It's looking bad and it's not getting any familiar folks," said Roger.

Wahoo Yahoo called out, "I'm out of water! Somebody help!" Sir Puffer flew and came along.

"I got you," he said as he grabbed Wahoo with his feet and flew away for more water somewhere.

CHAPTER 33

Close to the Finish Line

Whip was lying inside the wreckage. He got back up and noticed the finish line outside ahead. Pition slithered inside and found him.

"Are you alright, Whip?" he asked.

"Yeah," said Whip as he found the rocket on his wagon. "Stupid rocket!" He pulled it off and threw it away. Suddenly, coughs occurred behind them.

"Help!" it was Tubbs calling out and coughing in the smoke. "Angus! Arctics! Help me!" He coughed again. "I'm suffocating! Somebody get me out of here!"

"Tubbs! Talk to us, we're here!" Whip called out.

"Over here, dude!" Tubbs called as he saw Whip and he found him. Pition heard him, too. "Whip, Pition," said Tubbs. "Am I glad to see you guys?"

Tehran walked inside the wreckage to look for his son. "Whip, where are you?!" he asked. He moved through the smoke and found him with Pition and Tubbs.

"He's right here!" Pition called Tehran. Tehran moved to him and Whip.

"There you are, boys," Tehran said.

"Dad!" Whip said as he put his hands under the bar resting on Tubbs. "Help me lift this thing off of Tubbs!" Tehran helped with the lifting. Pition used strength in his head to lift up the A as it continued falling apart.

"Come on!" said Tubbs. "We're about to make the guy in last place get here." They kept lifting.

"Ladies and gentlemen," said Roger, "it looks like it's all over." The audience gasped.

Suddenly, Angus appeared sneaking through the wreckage with a wagon just ahead of it. Just then, Whip, Tehran, Pition, and Tubbs had just broken free with smoke all over their bodies. They came out with Whip's wagon.

"I can't believe my eyes, folks!" Roger exclaimed at the sight. "We have survivors."

Angus looked behind himself at the other racers. "Huh! Augh!" he whimpered as he rolled his wagon straight toward the finish line. The others caught up. Whip used one of his legs to push the wagon forward.

"Go for it, son," said Tehran as he pushed Whip ahead. Pition was with him.

"I'm riding with him!" he said. He and Whip caught up with Angus. It was the final duel for the trophy.

"That's some kid you got there, Teh," said Tubbs to Tehran.

"Well, not exactly, Tubbs," said Tehran. "He's no kid anymore."

"Now there are two wagons left," said Roger, "one from each team. One of them has to win."

The crowd shouted, "Go Whip! Go Whip! Go Whip!..." Whip used his magic ability to speed the wagon up fast as Angus could barely keep up. Whip ripped the finish line's ribbon. The entire crowd cheered for the winner.

CHAPTER 34

The Trophy

"**T**eam 47 wins!" shouted Roger. "We have Whip Psy and Pition Vipers in the same wagon. We shall award them the gold cup of the College Amusers." Whip and Pition climbed out of the wagon. Whip walked up the stairs and a man held the gold cup trophy. He gave it to Whip.

"Way to go, Whip!" exclaimed Pition as he slithered up to him. "That's the way we showed those Arctics who's boss!"

"That's right, Pit," said Whip. "We did it to it."

Tehran ran to his son at the stand. Tubbs followed him. Sir Puffer appeared in the crowd with Wahoo Yahoo in an ice chest. Wahoo lifted his head out and said, "How do you like that? Our team lost for the first time!"

"Relax, Wahoo," said Puffer. "There are other sports, you know."

Tehran ran up the stand. "Congratulations, son!" he said. "I'm so proud of you." He gave his son a hug, and Whip hugged him back.

"Thanks, Dad," he said.

Angus cleared his throat, standing by Whip. Whip turned to him.

"Congratulations, Whip," Angus said. "I could've done this better myself without cheating."

"The bet's off, Angus," said Whip. "But I think you owe *him* something." He pointed to Tubbs who was standing on the other side of the stand.

"Ayyyy-Jayyyy!" Tubbs bellowed his voice. Angus looked at him with a frightened look and then he smiled. Tubbs said, "Hi, it's me. The bear you let down."

"Hey, whoa, Tubbs!" said Angus. "Look, this was a misunderstanding."

"Mmrrrrh!" Tubbs growled. "You're going down like a fuzzy bag of fleas."

"What do you mean?" asked Angus. "All I was doing was trying to win." He tried to run away but Tubbs grabbed his tail.

"Uh huh," said Tubbs. "I always thought that you would be a good leader. We'll just meet back at the Arctic igloo taking applications." He lifted Angus up.

"Okay, okay, let go of me you big fat bag of blubber!" Angus said angrily.

"Time to get on the last tip of swinging!" Tubbs said as he started swinging Angus around him. He suddenly threw him high into the sky. Angus screamed as he rose up to the blimp.

"Look out there, folks!" said Roger as he witnessed Angus coming up. Angus popped a hole in the blimp.

"I'm swinging around nonstop!" Roger said.

"I suppose Angus is gonna have a crash landing with that," said Pition.

"Don't sweat it," said Whip. "We are the first to beat the Arctics once and for all."

The blimp deflated and headed down toward the audience's seat aisles. The crowd ran for their lives.

"It looks like I'm in a bad dream and it just won't quit," said Roger.

"That's right, Roger," said Richard Connors.

Somebody turned off the show on the television in a small house. It was a house with an otter couple in a place called Otterville. It was a small town that nobody ever noticed.

"Hey!" said Mr. Otter. "I enjoyed that channel of sports."

"It's already over, dear," said Mrs. Otter.

"Bull crap!" said Mr. Otter.

CHAPTER 35

The End of the Year

It was a long year in college. It was the first year for Whip, Bobi, Pition, and Fentruck. It was the only year for Tehran, so he could get a college degree. His new career is being a philosopher. His theory is that villainy exists in one who is a nemesis. That counted for the Arctics being nemeses to Whip.

It all passed. Tehran had ordered a graduation gown for getting out of college. The boys had only begun college in the university. It came to May 2003. Tehran was dressed in his gown as the boys were dressed in tuxedoes.

"You're going out already?" Whip asked his father. They were out by the parking lot walking on the sidewalk.

"Yes," said Tehran. "I'm done with college. All I needed was that degree."

"Here," said Whip as he held a giant cup-shaped present wrapped in purple wrapping paper topped with a blue bow. "I have something for you."

"Thanks, Whip," said Tehran as he grabbed the present. "What is it?"

"Well, you gotta open it to find out," said Whip.

Tehran ripped the wrapping paper open. Inside was the College Amusers' gold cup that Whip received from the triathlon. Tehran felt a feeling that made him weep.

"But—" he said, "this trophy is yours."

"I know, Dad," said Whip sighing. "But I'm giving it to you. Read the inscription."

Tehran looked at the message on a tan piece of paper on the trophy's pedestal and read it: "I may not be your little boy anymore that I used to be, but no matter what happens, I will always be your son." He smiled and he and Whip hugged each other.

Suddenly, on the benches by the front, Bobi, Pition, and Fentruck we're having an early dinner.

"Check this out, man!" Bobi called to the Psys. "I got a triple hamburger from the stand!" He took off the bun and gobbled up the patties one by one. "Mmm, beefy."

"I hadn't eaten for months," said Pition. "I had to constrict a whole barbecued chicken."

"Mm," said Fentruck, "this food of yours isn't bad at all. I miss eating shellfish."

Whip giggled about his friends. "Come on, Dad," he said. "Let's feast." He and his father walked toward the others, but suddenly, a car's horn was beeped in front of the walk. It was Whip's mother, Corbin, driving with Whip's kid sister, Sarah in the back. Corbin waved to her husband.

"Uh, actually, son," Tehran said, "I have my own plans if you're interested."

"Where are you all going?" Whip asked.

"Out somewhere nice for the summer," said Tehran. Whip followed him by the car.

"Hi, Mom," he said.

"How's college?" Corbin asked.

"It's excellent," said Whip.

"Are you gonna come with us, Whip?" asked Sarah.

"No," said Whip. "My friends and I are gonna do some major activities."

"You might understand when you're old like him, Sarah," Corbin said. "We're going out to the east coast," she said to Whip.

"Well, I'm really gonna miss you, family," said Whip.

Tehran sat in the front passenger's seat with the gold cup. "Whip received this trophy in these 'Amusers' competitions with a diabolical team called the Arctics," he said.

"Interesting," said Corbin.

"I have Fredwick to keep me company," Sarah said as she held onto her stuffed toy dragon. "Too bad Whip won't come with us."

"It's all right, Sarah," said Whip. "Practical adults like me can do anything they want."

"Bye, Whip," said Tehran.

"Bye," said Whip, waving to his family as they drove away. He giggled and said, "That is so my kind." He rejoined his friends.

As the rest of the Psy family drove among grassy hills on the road, Tehran had a thought.

"What do you say we go for...?" he asked.

"Something like a picnic?" Corbin said.

"That water might be too cold to swim," said Sarah.

"You'll get used to that, honey," said Corbin.

"You know," said Tehran, "my philosophy states that a psyvark can do anything at all in this world." They drove so and so far to the east coast.

AMUSERS' IDOL

elcome to the College Amusers' Idol, a karaoke contest for geniuses only! It's up to our host Gaston Sexton to crown the next Amusers' Idol.

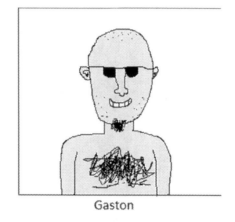

Gaston

First off today is Whip Psy. He is singing "I'll Be" by Edwin McCain.

Gaston: "That's an interesting solo, NEXT!"
Bobi: "It's gator time! Pm ba doo, Pm ba doo."
Bobi is singing "Wishing Well" by Terence Trent D'Arby.

Bobi: (After singing the chorus) "That's right I'm a crocodile of cheers, man!"

Gaston: "What a genius. Next singer!"

Music starts. Pition is singing "Everything I Do (I Do It For You)" by Bryan Adams.

Gaston: "Nice solo. I didn't know snakes could sing."

Fentruck is next; he is singing "Don't Worry Be Happy" by Bobby McFerrin. Whistling goes on.

Gaston: "What a wonderful walrus.
Next is Beau Fraîche. She is singing "I'm the Only One" by Melissa Etheridge.

Gaston: "She is a talented singer. Those lessons work out great for her."
Next is the big brown bear. He is singing "Sweet Caroline" by Neil Diamond.

A cane pulls in and grabs the bear by the neck. Next is "Pageboy" Landon Baines. He is singing "Uptown Girl" by Billy Joel.

"AUGH!"

A trap door opens under him.

Bobi: "I always thought he was sexy."

Next is the living skeleton. It is singing "Bad to the Bone" by George Thorogood and the Destroyers.

A hammer falls and knocks the skeleton apart.

Gaston: "Okay, that was retarded."

Next, we have Angus Wellington, Jr. He is singing "How's It Gonna Be" by Third Eye Blind.

"AUGH!"

A spring from the back wall jumps out and bounces Angus off the stage.

Gaston: "After all, that guy is vanquished."

Gavin from high school skates by and walks up to the stage and asks, "Is this singing I hear around here?"

Whip: "It sure is."

Gaston: "I didn't hire a punk kid to come here."

Gavin: "Let me sing, I've got talent."

Whip: "Alright, go ahead."

Music starts loud. Gavin is singing the theme song of the "Pokémon" TV series.

Whip: "Wow!"

Bobi: "It's amazing how he just came up with all the words in the Pokémon theme. What a genius."

Now who'll be named the College Amusers' next idol? Will it be...

Pition Vipers
(see c)

Whip Psy (see a)   Bobert Gatorson (see b)

Fentruck Tusker (see d)

Beau Fraîche
(see e)

The Big Brown Bear
(see f)

"Pageboy" Landon
Baines (see g)

The Living
Skeleton (see h)

Angus Wellington, Jr.
(see i)

Gavin Harding
(see j)

OR   ? Now it's your turn to vote. Select your favorite.

Gaston: "And the next Amusers' Idol is…"

   a. "Whip, of course." Sing along with the song he sings.
   b. "Bobi." Sing the song.
   c. "Our little snake friend, Pition." Sing the song.
   d. "Our walrus pal, Fentruck." Sing the song.

e. "Nope, unacceptable."
f. "Impossible, I won't allow it."
g. "<Laughing> No. You're being ridiculous."
h. "Nope. Better luck next time."
i. "Pa-hah! You've got to be kidding me."
j. "Negative. Go fish if you don't have cards."

If you select losers, it's Gaston's turn to sing.

Gaston: "What do you know? It's me, everyone."

Music beats. Gaston is singing "Pour Some Sugar On Me" by Def Leppard.

Ladies and gentlemen, our time is up for the idol, so good luck reading the next adventures of Whip.

Other books by Tyler Johns:
Whip Books:
Whip
Whip 2: Whip's Christmas Adventure

The Sharp Empire books:
The Sharp Empire
The Sharp Empire II: The Serpent Strikes Back
The Sharp Empire III: The Phantom of the Galaxy
The Sharp Empire IV: Return of the Gospel

Coming Soon: Whip 4: Whip Goes to Mars